THE
BACHELORS
of BLACKWATER
LAKE

SPECIAL EDITION

Just a Little Bit Married

Teresa Southwick

HARLEQUIN

SPECIAL EDITION

Life, Love & Family.

AVAILABLE THIS MONTH

#2533 FORTUNE'S SECOND-CHANCE COWBOY
The Fortunes of Texas: The Secret Fortunes
Marie Ferrarella

#2534 JUST A LITTLE BIT MARRIED
The Bachelors of Blackwater Lake
Teresa Southwick

#2535 KISS ME, SHERIFF!
The Men of Thunder Mountain
Wendy Warren

#2536 THE MARINE MAKES HIS MATCH
Camden Family Secrets
Victoria Pade

#2537 PREGNANT BY MR. WRONG
The McKinnels of Jewell Rock
Rachael Johns

#2538 A FAMILY UNDER THE STARS
Sugar Falls, Idaho
Christy Jeffries

EAN

HSEATMIFC0317

"Don't expect me to forgive you," she said.

"I don't." But seeing her again, remembering that they'd once been two halves of a whole, made him wish she could. "I just thought you should know about the divorce."

"It is kind of important," she agreed. "Chances are I would have found out the hard way pretty soon."

"Oh?"

"I've been dating someone and it's getting serious." She turned away and walked over to the couch, absently rearranging throw pillows. "Lately he's been hinting about getting married."

Linc had absolutely no right to the feeling, but that didn't stop the blast of raw jealousy that roared through him. "I guess it would have been awkward to apply for a marriage license and find out you were still married."

"You think?"

He detected the tiniest bit of defensiveness in her voice and decided to take a shot. "You never told him you'd been married before?"

"We were married for fifteen minutes." Ten years ago her eyes took on shades of gray when she was annoyed, and they looked that way now. "It was a long time ago. I've been busy. It didn't seem important."

"The thing is, you never checked to find out about the divorce," he reminded her.

"Neither did you."

"Fair enough. I'll take care of it now..."

THE BACHELORS OF BLACKWATER LAKE:
They won't be single for long!

Dear Reader,

Do you remember the first time you fell in love? The soul-searing, fill-your-senses-with-magic kind when all you could think about was that person and being with them? It's a once-in-a-lifetime thrill. But thinking with your heart isn't always best and can lead to painful decisions, leaving deep wounds that never heal and cause lifelong regret. *If only* are arguably the most profoundly sad two words in the English language.

But what if you got a do-over?

In *Just a Little Bit Married*, Lincoln Hart finds himself in this position. Ten years ago he was a blissfully happy newlywed who learned a family secret—one he believed could hurt the woman he loved more than his own life. To protect her he got a divorce, or so he thought. The papers were never filed and he has a chance for, if not making things right, at least earning redemption.

Rose Tucker is struggling—and failing—to make her interior-design business a success. The last thing she needs is a personal problem, but that's what she gets when the man who sliced and diced her heart shows up to tell her they're still married. Worse, he offers her a high-profile job decorating his condo. To save her business she has to accept it and his help. But what if her first love also turns out to be her last?

One of my favorite things about being a writer is playing "what if." In chapter one of a book there are an infinite number of directions to take your characters. I hope you enjoy the direction of Linc and Rose's story of first love, one that neither of them ever got over.

Happy reading!

Teresa Southwick

Just a Little Bit Married

Teresa Southwick

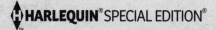

Recycling programs
for this product may
not exist in your area.

ISBN-13: 978-0-373-62333-4

Just a Little Bit Married

Copyright © 2017 by Teresa Southwick

Printed in U.S.A.

Teresa Southwick lives with her husband in Las Vegas, the city that reinvents itself every day. An avid fan of romance novels, she is delighted to be living out her dream of writing for Harlequin.

Visit the Author Profile page
at Harlequin.com for more titles.

To my sister-in-law, Rose Boyle.
I borrowed your name for the heroine in this book
because she's as smart and sweet as you.
Thanks for marrying my brother, sole sister!

Chapter One

"Rose, this might come as a shock, but we're not divorced."

Lincoln Hart looked around the room to make sure there was nothing pointed, heavy, or sharp enough to take out an eye, bash in his skull or maim a fairly important body part. Satisfied, he studied the woman he hadn't seen in ten years and realized Rose Tucker was even more beautiful than she'd been then, when she took his breath away every time he saw her. When he was so in love that being apart from her was almost a physical ache.

Rose. Even her name was lovely. She was more polished than the young woman he'd walked away from. And more hostile, but he couldn't blame her.

After what he'd just said she was going to hate him even more than she had a decade ago, and she'd hated him quite a lot then.

"What? Not even a hello?" The hostility in her dark blue eyes wavered to make way for surprise, then suspicion.

"I thought it best to lead with the headline, make sure you got the information before slamming the door in my face."

"You're telling me we're still married? I don't believe you. What kind of game are you playing now? What in the world would you have to gain by pretending we're still married?"

"I'm not pretending. And I'm as thrown by this as you are."

"I doubt that." She put a hand to her forehead as if feeling dizzy.

Linc reached out and curved his fingers around her upper arm to steady her. "Let's sit down."

Apparently his touch snapped her out of it because she yanked her arm away. He half expected her to take a swing at him and wouldn't blame her if she did. This whole mess was his fault from start to finish. If there was anything at all positive about his screwup, it was that his family knew nothing about his brief, whirlwind marriage.

His brothers, Sam and Cal, would rag on him relentlessly, which was bad enough. Katherine and Hastings Hart, his mother and her husband, and his younger sister, Ellie, would be disappointed in him for the way he'd handled the situation. But none of that mattered now. He and Rose had a problem and it was all on him.

"We should probably sit—"

"Don't be nice to me, Linc. We both know that's not who you are."

"What I did to you was lousy, Rose, but that's not who I am." He wasn't the man she thought she'd married, but he wasn't a complete jerk, either.

They stood in the postage-stamp-sized living area of her apartment, which was upstairs from her small interior design studio in an old, redbrick building on one of Prosper,

Texas's, side streets. The fact that this one-room place had charm was a reflection of her skill as an interior designer. The paint was pale gold except for one olive-green accent wall in the living room. The kitchen and living areas were set apart by the clever placement of the love-seat-sized sofa. Wall hangings, knickknacks, lamps and throw pillows added color without being stuffy and formal. It was homey and warm. He liked her taste very much.

"You must have questions," he said.

"How do you know we're not divorced?" She tucked a strand of long black hair behind her ear.

"My lawyer passed away after a short illness and I had to hire a new one to handle my personal affairs. He insisted on looking over all of my official documents. There was a marriage license but no divorce decree. After researching the situation, he discovered that the papers were never filed with the court."

"How could that happen?"

It was hard not to cringe at her bewildered tone, especially since he'd assured her he would handle everything. "I hired a half-price lawyer and got what I paid for—half a divorce."

"Why would you do that, Linc? Your family is worth millions and Hart Industries must have a platoon of the best and brightest legal minds around. It doesn't make sense that you would get an attorney from outside the company, especially someone incompetent. The Harts don't do things like that."

Leave it to Rose to zero in on the core of the problem. It wasn't something he wanted to talk about, but she had a right to know. "I'm not a Hart."

"Excuse me? You're what now?"

"Hastings Hart isn't my father."

"No way." She shook her head.

"It's true. Hastings and Katherine confirmed it. I found out right after we got married."

"How?"

"My biological father came to see me. He confessed he had a…thing with my mother."

"You told me your parents were deliriously happy," Rose said with equal amounts of accusation and defensiveness in her voice.

"That was their story. Turns out there was a rough patch. My older brothers were born nine months apart—twins the hard way, she always said. The fact is she had her hands full raising them and Hastings wasn't around much. He was traveling, working long hours to build Hart Industries into something he could leave to his sons."

"So she turned to another man and had an affair?"

"He and my mother were legally separated and headed for a divorce, so technically it wasn't an extramarital affair."

"And you never knew? Never suspected?" There was skepticism in the questions.

"No. They worked through their problems and he promised to give me his name. Both of them agreed there was no reason for me to know."

"And your biological father was all right with the arrangement?"

"He was a lawyer on the partner track at an ultraconservative law firm that specialized in divorce. Sleeping with a client and getting her pregnant would have caused a scandal that might have cost him his career, so keeping it secret was fine with him."

"Yet he told you all those years later. Why?"

"Midlife crisis, I guess. He never had children." He stopped, waiting for the anger to roll through him so he could continue the act and pretend he was reconciled to the ugly secret. "No one to carry on the family name got to him, probably."

"You don't know?"

"It was a short conversation. At that moment I didn't know whether or not he was lying." Turned out the guy was the only one who *hadn't* lied. "Hastings and Katherine confirmed."

"And you haven't talked to your father since? Asked him why he finally came forward?"

"No." The man ruined his life. Sharing DNA didn't make that okay. "The narcissistic bastard only thought about the fact that he had a son, not what the revelation would do to that son."

"Oh, God. Linc—" Shock and resentment were replaced by pity in her eyes and that wasn't much of an improvement. "I guess it hit you hard."

"Let's just say finding out your parents lied to you about Santa Claus is nothing compared to learning your father isn't who you thought." Linc had had no idea who he was and his only thought was to protect Rose, even from himself.

He remembered that time as if it was yesterday. She'd been hired for the summer at Hart Industries in the real-estate development branch of the company he was taking over. They fell madly in love, had a whirlwind romance and he swept her away to Las Vegas, where they got married. It was the best time of his life and he'd never been happier. Then everything went to hell.

He shook his head and met her gaze. "You thought you married a Hart but I'm not one."

Understanding dawned in her eyes. "You think that was important to me?"

Intensity rotated through him and was nearly as powerful as what he'd felt ten years ago. He recalled the anguish and pain in her voice when she'd pleaded with him to tell her why he was leaving. What she'd done. It was an understatement to say he hadn't been thinking clearly. He left the Harts, too, and stayed away for a long time. "It mattered to me."

"So you had to split from me and got a half-price lawyer to do it."

"I didn't feel it was right to use a Hart attorney since I wasn't really part of the family. And in the spirit of full disclosure, I walked away from everyone." He backpacked through Europe, although it would be more accurate to say that he drank his way from one country to the next. "After two years I came back." But he never forgot that he was the bastard son who always needed to prove himself.

"And your father? The biological one?"

"What about him?"

"What's he like?"

"Good question. Like I said, I don't see him. And if it's all the same to you I don't want to talk about him. I only brought it up for context."

"Don't expect me to forgive you," she said.

"I don't." But seeing her again, remembering that they'd once been two halves of a whole, made him wish she could. "I just thought you should know about the divorce."

"It is kind of important," she agreed. "Chances are I would have found out the hard way pretty soon."

"Oh?"

"I've been dating someone and it's getting serious." She turned away and walked over to the couch, absently re-arranging throw pillows. "Lately he's been hinting about getting married."

Linc had absolutely no right to the feeling but that didn't stop the blast of raw jealousy that roared through him. "I guess it would have been awkward to apply for a marriage license and find out you were still married."

"You think?"

He detected the tiniest bit of defensiveness in her voice and decided to take a shot. "You never told him you'd been married before?"

"We were married for fifteen minutes." Ten years ago her eyes took on shades of gray when she was annoyed and they looked that way now. "It was a long time ago. I've been busy. It didn't seem important."

"The thing is, you never checked to find out about the divorce," he reminded her.

"Neither did you."

"Fair enough. I will take care of it now. Mason, my new lawyer, will handle the details and send the papers to you for your signature. Then it will be behind us." At least the paperwork part. His feelings were a lot more complicated than he'd expected.

"Okay." She frowned. "How did you know where I was?"

"How does anyone find anyone? I looked you up on the internet."

Also he'd checked her out, found out what she'd been doing all these years. First college, then five years working with a prestigious design firm in Dallas before opening her own business not quite two years ago. And it wasn't doing well. If she was, she'd still be located in Dallas, not thirty-five miles away, where office and living spaces were combined and cheap.

She ran everything herself, no hired help and therefore no payroll. There were a few flooring, window-covering and paint samples in her downstairs studio, but not what you'd see in a larger, successful company.

Her reputation was good, but her business was going

down with a whimper. Unless someone gave her a high-profile opportunity.

"Look, Rose, there's another reason I came to see you."

"What else could there possibly be? Isn't the fact that we're not legally divorced enough?"

"This is a good thing. Trust me."

"Seriously? You have the nerve to ask me to trust you? Getting involved with you was the worst mistake of my life."

"Right." He refused to react, to let her know the arrow hit its mark. "You have no reason to trust me. And that doesn't bode well, because I want to offer you a job."

"Doing what?"

"Decorating." He moved closer. "My condo in Blackwater Lake, Montana."

"And why would I want to do that?"

"Because the town is about to be on the rich-and-famous radar when a new hotel, condo and retail project opens. The hotel is entering the last phase of construction and will need decorating. I know the developer. Use my condo for your résumé and dazzle them. I'll put in a good word." Linc pitched her the rest of the details, then asked, "What do you think?"

"I think I want to know what your angle is."

"No ulterior motive." Except giving her business a helping hand might earn him some redemption points.

"I don't need your charity."

"That's not what this is." He slid his fingertips into the pockets of his slacks. "I don't deserve a favor, but I'm asking for one. Just think about it."

"Why?"

"Because you're good at what you do." He pulled a card from his wallet and set it on the coffee table. "Call me in a few days with your decision. And before you think about *not* calling, you should know that I'll contact you."

"Okay."

Linc was reluctant to leave but decided not to push his luck. The weird thing was he'd never planned to offer her a job. That changed when he saw her.

Accepting his proposition would mean traveling to Blackwater Lake with him and he really wanted her to do that. For old time's sake. For her business. To make things up to her so he would feel better about what he'd done.

Ultimately the reasons were about him, which did, in fact, make him a self-centered bastard like his father.

"What do you mean you're married? More important—why do I not know this about you? And don't even get me started on why I wasn't invited to the wedding."

Rose stared at her BFF, Vicki Jeffers. After Linc left she couldn't stop shaking. He was a ghost from the past and she'd barely held it together when he showed up out of the blue. She'd really needed to talk to someone and begged her friend to come over. Apparently her shocked and shaky tone had convinced the other woman to break a date. So Rose told her story and the other woman was now staring at her as if she had two heads.

"I'm not married so much as not quite divorced." She took another sip of the wine Vicki had brought. It was a nice vintage, more than Rose could afford. The business she'd launched eighteen months ago wasn't exactly setting the world on fire. Paying her bills was a challenge and left no room in the budget for an expensive bottle of cabernet.

"So you've been married for ten years."

"Not technically," Rose objected.

"Yeah, technically," Vicki countered. "Because if you're

not divorced, you're still married. And you just said that happened almost ten years ago."

"It ended after a nanosecond, so not really married that long."

"Might not feel that way but legally you've been his wife all these years." Vicki sighed and held up a hand. She was sitting at the other end of the couch and tucked her legs up beside her, settling in for a marathon heart-to-heart. "Why don't you start at the beginning?"

Rose blew out a long breath as the highs and lows of that emotional time tumbled through her mind. "It was the summer before I started college. I got a clerical job at Hart Industries. Lincoln Hart had just finished his master's degree in business and was taking his place in the company his father started." Although now she knew Hastings Hart wasn't his biological father.

"So... What? He hit on you? Used his position of power to sexually harass you?"

"Why would you think such a thing?"

"Because I'm a lawyer," Vicki said.

"A very cynical one." Rose shook her head. "He was a perfect gentleman. The truth is we fell madly in love and got married."

"And you never saw fit to say a word about it when we met at school? I thought we shared all of our secrets." There was just a tinge of hurt in her friend's brown eyes. Vicki wrapped a long strand of silky blond hair around her finger and stared accusingly. "But you kept the secret that you were Rose Hart."

The name had a nice ring to it, but she'd never even had a chance to change the last name on her driver's license. "Linc abruptly ended things and said he would handle the divorce details and a lawyer would contact me if he needed anything from me. No one did, so I thought it was done."

"And you didn't wonder why you never heard anything about signing the settlement papers?"

"What did I know about a divorce?" And if she was being honest, there'd been a lot of denial going on. And she'd been so hurt. The pain of not being with him was almost more than she could bear. So many awful feelings. The shock of being dumped without an explanation. Overwhelming bewilderment. Now she knew what happened but still didn't understand why he had to leave her. She would have done anything for Lincoln Hart—or whatever his name was. "I was practically a baby."

"You weren't too young to get married."

"He swept me off my feet. I couldn't say no to him. And he—"

"What?" Vicki's eyes narrowed. "Did he do something?"

"Not what you're probably thinking. He was incredibly sweet and understanding." Not to mention sexy and handsome and completely irresistible. Unfortunately the "sexy and handsome" part hadn't changed. But he was totally resistible to her now. "I was a virgin."

Vicki nearly choked on her wine. "How is that possible?"

"You make me sound like a weirdo. I was only eighteen."

"And crazy in love," Vicki reminded her. "You just told me that you couldn't say no."

"To marriage," she amended. "My mom drilled into me that a man has no need to buy the cow when he gets the milk for free. And if you give it away, he'll just mosey on down the road to another cow. That's what happened to her. Unfortunately when my father moseyed, she was stuck with a baby." Rose pointed to herself. "Yours truly."

"Ah."

"She was determined that the same thing wouldn't happen to me and never let up with the warning not to sleep with a man until I had a ring on my finger. I thought I got really lucky that the man of my dreams was determined to marry me. Of course I couldn't say no."

"So he married you to…" Vicki tapped her lips. "Pop your cherry?"

"That's what I believed for ten years." Rose recalled every word of what he'd said before walking out of her life. She remembered him telling her that he couldn't be with her because he wasn't in her league. She'd thought that was about him having more money than God and her not fitting into his world. Now she knew he'd been talking about himself because his father wasn't who he'd thought. "He had a crisis of identity."

Vicki rolled her eyes. "Yeah, I can see how that could happen. Must be tough figuring out which billions belong to you or your brothers when you're a Hart."

That's just it. At the time he'd recently learned he wasn't biologically a part of the family. But she didn't feel comfortable revealing that.

"Things aren't always what they seem." Rose knew that statement was cryptic, but it wasn't her secret to share, not even with the friend who was like a sister to her.

"A case could be made," Vicki said pointedly, "that he proposed because he was after one thing. Correct me if I'm wrong, but he got what he wanted, then said adios."

"You're not wrong." But there was more to it.

"And you're not divorced? Seems to me someone from the legal department at Hart Industries should be canned over this."

"You'd think." Rose shrugged. "It's probably not a stretch to say that my vow of chastity could have impacted the haste of his proposal. But, I am my mother's daughter." Although she'd made up her mind to be different from Janie Tucker and not play the victim card for the rest of her life.

"So, how was it?" Vicki sipped the last of the wine in her glass. "Seeing him again, I mean?"

"It was surreal. He hasn't changed, other than being ten years older. But it looks good on him." And she hated that. If he was fat, bald and irritating the trauma of having her heart ripped out and handed back would have been worth it. But her luck wasn't that good.

His eyes were still a mesmerizing shade of dark blue. He was tall, lean and broad-shouldered. Walking, talking animal magnetism that was so powerful she could hardly remember what she'd said to him. "And, darn him, like all men he just looks better. Call me shallow, but this would be so much easier if he looked like a troll."

"Very annoying of him." Vicki shifted her position on the couch. "Were there still sparks between you?"

Not unless anger counted. Or maybe it never went away. It had been hard, but ten years ago she pulled herself together and patched the hole Linc left in her life. There was a good possibility that anger had filled up that empty space. "Nope. No sparks."

"So, he came to personally inform you that your divorce never happened." Her friend tilted her head. "That means your tenth wedding anniversary is coming up soon."

"Since we haven't lived together, I don't think there will be an exchange of gifts." Sarcasm was good, Rose thought. It was a sign that she was rebounding.

"I wonder what you give for ten years of marriage."

"A divorce, hopefully." Yay her. A pithy comeback. She was on a roll.

Vicki shook her head, still trying to take in the situation. "How could you never tell me about all this?"

"Haven't you ever done something that is so completely mortifying and humiliating that you didn't want anyone to know about it ever?"

"Of course." Her friend grinned. "But nothing this spectacular. And you know all of my mortifying and humiliating escapades. Yet you kept this to yourself."

"I'm sorry."

"No, no. Don't give me those big, blue Kewpie-doll eyes. You're only sorry you got caught. I want to know why I didn't hear about this until crisis time."

"At first I just wanted to forget. Start college and put it behind me." She'd thought not talking about it would make the pain go away but she'd been wrong. Time had been the cure. "You and I met, and clicked, but I didn't really know you that well. Then the longer I didn't say anything, the more I didn't know how to bring it up. Besides, I thought I was quietly divorced and no one ever had to know."

If no one knew, it wouldn't hurt as bad, right?

"Speaking of that… It's probably a good thing that you found out. Otherwise, when you and Chandler went to get a marriage license, that could have been a shock," Vicki commented.

"That's what Linc said."

"Good. He knows you haven't been pining for him."

If she'd never seen him again Rose would accept that as true. But the rush of emotions when she'd answered her door and instantly recognized him stirred memories of that brief, shining moment when she'd had everything she ever wanted. Had there been pining going on and she wasn't aware of it?

Vicki set her empty glass on the coffee table. "How did Chandler take this 'being married and not divorced' thing?"

"He doesn't know."

"You haven't told him yet?" Her friend looked more shocked about that than any revelation so far.

"No."

"Keeping important details to yourself is starting to form a disturbing pattern. Why haven't you told him?"

"It just happened a few hours ago," Rose protested.

"You called me. It's not a stretch that you could have clued Chandler in on this."

"I needed to wrap my head around it before dumping this kind of news on him. And—" Rose loved her friend, but this rational side could be annoying. Mostly because Vicki was right. "The situation got even more complicated."

"I don't see how."

"Linc offered me a job decorating his condo. A very high-profile project that will generate a lot of attention and publicity."

"There's more, right?" her friend asked suspiciously.

"If it goes well, there's a chance I could get more work in the area. These guys—the Holdens—are building a hotel and resort, all of which will need decorating. This is a once-in-a-lifetime opportunity."

"Obviously you didn't say no."

"You're a lawyer. If someone offered you a case that was the equivalent of this, would you walk away from it? No matter who was doing the asking?"

"I see your point," Vicki reluctantly agreed.

"This could be really lucrative. A career maker." She filled in even more details about the development and the area with luxury homes cropping up. "We both know if I don't get a break Tucker Designs is finished."

"Maybe not—"

Rose's look stopped the words. "I'm going down, Vee. You're my attorney. You've seen my financials. I don't even want to think about that loan from the small business association. And then there's my mom. She raised me completely by herself and worked so hard all her life to take care of me. Waitressing isn't easy and I'd like her to be able to cut back. Enjoy herself more. You know?"

"Yes, but—" Vicki stopped and shook her head.

"How do you think Chandler would take it?" Rose asked.

"Let me think about this." Vicki hummed the *Jeopardy* theme. "You tell the man you're all but engaged to that you're going to Montana with the man you married ten years ago and aren't quite divorced from to do a job in order to save your business."

Rose nodded. "Yes."

"I think any man's head would explode given that scenario."

"That's what I figured, too." This was what Rose really wanted to talk to her friend about. She'd revealed her history with Linc because it had a direct bearing on her decision. As Linc would say—context. "What do you think I should do?"

It didn't take Vicki very long to come up with an answer. "Tell Chandler and don't take the job."

Rose nearly choked on her wine. That's not what she'd expected. "What? I thought you understood."

"I do. But I also saw your face when you talked about Lincoln Hart." There was sympathy in her friend's expression. "I've known you for a long time and you've never looked like that before. Tell me I'm nuts but whether you're willing to admit it or not, you have feelings for the man."

"Of course I do. All of them bad."

"Take it from me. Accepting that job will dredge up more feelings and all the crap comes up, too. Just leave it alone. You're doing fine. Don't give him a chance to hurt you again."

"He can't."

"Okay." Vicki's tone was full of "if you say so but I think you're wrong." "For what it's worth, my advice is to talk this over with Chandler. I'm sure he'll tell you the same thing. Do not take this job."

"Wow, don't hold back. Tell me how you really feel."

"I always do." Her friend smiled. "And just so you know, I want to look over those divorce papers before you sign anything. This time things will run smoothly or you'll know why."

"Thank you, Vicki."

"So you're not mad at me?"

"Why would I be?" Rose protested.

"For telling you what I thought. I know you didn't want to hear that."

"I count on you."

"So we're okay?" her friend asked.

"Absolutely."

That was completely true and Rose valued this woman's opinion more than she could say. But she was going to break the unbreakable rule about automatically taking your best friend's advice. Rose just hoped there wouldn't be an "I told you so" in her future.

Chapter Two

"So you're really moving to Blackwater Lake, Montana?"

Linc was standing by the side table in his office, where there was a bottle of exceptional single malt Scotch, and glanced over his shoulder. It was precisely six thirty and Mason Archer, his attorney, stood in the doorway. Right on time.

"Would you like a drink?" Linc asked.

"Yes." The other man walked closer, passing the desk piled with papers, and went directly to the conversation area with its leather furniture and sleek glass-and-chrome coffee table.

After handing Mason the tumbler of Scotch, Linc said, "You know my sister, Ellie, lives there, right?"

"I do."

Linc grinned because there was no missing his friend's clipped tone. "Don't take her rejection personally."

"How do you take it when a woman says there's nothing that could compel her to have dinner with you?"

"That was a bad time. She'd been burned and swore off men," Linc said. Mason had worked for Hart Industries while Ellie was still there. The man once had a thing for her but that was before she met her husband. However, bringing it up never failed to get a rise out of his friend. Linc liked to get a rise out of him because it almost never happened. "Trust me, it wasn't personal."

"Okay."

"That's it? You're a lawyer who makes arguments for a living. It's like air to you."

"Knowing when not to argue is just as important. Ellie is happily married and has a child. I'm glad for her."

"So you're over her," Linc persisted.

"There was never anything to get over."

"If you say so."

Mason sighed before taking a sip of his drink. "There are many, many other clients I could work for."

"You'd lose a lot of money if you left me," Linc reminded him.

"The peace and quiet would be worth it." Tough words but the other man was smiling.

"You're going to miss me when I'm in Montana."

"Tell me again why it is that you're going," his friend said.

"I'm buying in to my brother-in-law's construction company. It needs an infusion of capital to expand in Blackwater Lake. The town is one of the fastest growing places in the country and there's a lot of opportunity."

The one at the top of his list was getting out of the Hart family shadow. He'd insisted on being treated as an employee of the company and not an heir apparent, like his half brothers. In the last ten years he'd worked his ass off, partly to prove himself to them and partly to stay too busy to think about how his personal life had imploded. The other day he'd seen the anger and resentment in Rose's eyes but that was better than having her grow to despise him because he wasn't a Hart.

He didn't tell her because she would have said she fell in love with the man and not his last name. But the truth was it would have been like marrying the prince who would be king, then finding out he'd been switched at birth for the peasant who owned a pigsty. Walking away saved her from having to deal with that. It was the right thing to do but that didn't get him off the restitution hook for how he'd treated her.

The upside of keeping too busy to brood over lost love was making a lot of money. And he was going to take that money to Blackwater Lake and build more success on his own terms.

Linc remembered telling Rose that it was about to be on the "rich and famous" radar. A place for her to build success too but he had yet to hear from her. It was amazing how much that bugged him. And it's not like he hadn't known there was a better-than-even chance she would tell him to stick his offer where the sun didn't shine.

"Opportunity in rural Montana?" Mason drained the rest of the Scotch in his glass. "There's nowhere to go but up when you're in the sticks."

"It has an airport now." A thought popped into Linc's mind. "You should think about opening a law office there."

"I'm not licensed to practice in Montana."

"You could be. It's probably not a big deal to make that happen." Linc sat on the leather love seat. "There's no competition right now. Could be a good move for you, my friend."

"Not so bad for you, either." The attorney's tone was wry.

This man was an outstanding lawyer. Principled, meticulous, conscientious and smart. They'd met while working for Hart Industries, then Mason had opened his own law firm. When Linc's personal attorney passed away Mason was the guy he wanted. "I'll admit having legal counsel close by would be convenient, but your success and happiness are a concern."

Mason laughed. That was worth mentioning because it didn't happen often. He was far too serious. Linc figured a woman would find him good-looking and wondered what Rose would think. For a split second there was a white-hot flash of jealousy. Not unlike the feeling he'd experienced when she'd mentioned dating someone and that it was getting serious. Again he had a flicker of annoyance at her not getting back to him about the job offer.

"Seriously?" The other man set his empty glass on the silver tray beside the Scotch bottle. "My happiness?"

"Blackwater Lake is a great place. Nice people. Beautiful scenery. Lots to do all year round with the lake and the mountains. You could have a hand in shaping its growth in a positive way. And do something good for yourself at the same time."

Mason's eyes narrowed. "Correct me if I'm wrong, but didn't you once call it Black Hole, Montana?"

"That was a different time."

Linc remembered it well. Ellie had called him, upset because she was pregnant and things were not going well between her and the baby's father, Alex McKnight. The man had eventually won over Linc as well as Sam and Cal. He married Ellie and they had a daughter, Leah, who was two. Moving to the small town in Montana was the best thing ever, she often said to him. Now he was going to see whether or not she was right.

"So, Mason, before we grab dinner, you're probably wondering how the meeting went."

"I'm assuming you're talking about the one with your wife," the attorney clarified.

That took Linc by surprise. The wife part. It had been ten years and as Rose had pointed out, they were married for fifteen minutes. Not nearly long enough to think about her being his wife. Regret about that coiled inside him. And in the decade that had passed no woman had gotten close to him again. Ellie had said more than once that he used women like cocktail napkins and threw them away because he'd never fallen in love. The truth was exactly the opposite. Because he'd loved so deeply and had to let her go he wouldn't ever risk it a second time.

"Linc?"

"Yeah. Right. How did it go with Rose." He shook his head to clear it and thought for a moment. "Better than I expected."

Mason waited, then finally said, "Care to give me the highlights?"

"She didn't throw anything."

"You were at her place." It wasn't a question.

Since Linc hadn't given him the when and where, he asked, "How did you know?"

"She didn't want to break any of her stuff."

"Ah." He hadn't thought of that when picking the venue for his bombshell. His only thought had been that the last thing she'd ever said to him was that she never wanted to see him again. There wouldn't have been a meeting if he'd tried to set one up. Surprise had been the only option. And it worked, sort of. He'd expected to feel nothing and got a surprise of his own at the flood of emotion, the explosion of memories that was like being pelted with hail.

"And after she didn't throw anything?" Mason prompted. "What did she say?"

"She didn't believe it." Linc had revealed everything

to his attorney, including the fact that Hastings Hart was not his biological father. "I explained what happened and convinced her it was true. Of course she wanted to know how the divorce screwup happened."

"You get what you pay for." There was an ironic tone in the other man's voice.

"I already told you that was before your time. Rose seemed...sympathetic after I told her about what happened."

Sympathy was so much more palatable than pity. And he would never be sure whether or not his standing in a financial dynasty mattered to her because he'd taken that choice out of her hands. It was impossible to know for sure if she fell in love with *him*, or the him that was part of the Hart family fiscal package. But in the last ten years he'd learned women were attracted to money even when it came from a bastard.

"What did she say?"

Linc met the other man's gaze. "That I should have told her what was going on."

"You have no idea how hard it is for me not to say 'duh.'"

"Don't think I didn't notice you just did." Linc sighed. "No one is disputing the fact that I'm an ass."

"It's not too late to change."

"Sometimes it is."

"You're ten years older and wiser," Mason reminded him.

"True. But age and wisdom can't undo what I did to her. Only reparation can do that."

"It's true that I haven't worked for you long, but I'm sensing something." Mason's attorney expression returned. "Did she mention retaining legal counsel?"

"No."

"She should," Mason pointed out. "To protect her rights."

"I have no intention of treating her unfairly in the divorce settlement."

The other man's eyes narrowed. "Then what did you do?"

"I offered her a job."

"Doing what?"

Linc hadn't shared his research on Rose. "She has an interior-design business and it's not doing well. She needs some help."

"So, you're giving her money?" There was no approval or judgment in the other man's voice, he was just seeking clarification of facts.

"No. I want to hire her to decorate my place in Blackwater Lake. With the possibility of future high-profile projects to strengthen her résumé and get more work."

Mason thought that over, then nodded approvingly. "Smart move. Keep her happy to avoid an ugly and public divorce. In the long run a goodwill gesture could be less expensive than a lawsuit for retroactive alimony. Alienation of affection."

"This has nothing to do with dodging back–spousal support. She's entitled to a generous settlement." Pain and suffering came to mind and Linc winced. He hated that he was the one who'd hurt her. "But you should know that she hasn't agreed to my offer yet."

It had been long enough and Linc was beginning to wonder if Rose planned to ignore his proposition. He wasn't sure what constituted a decent length of time to allow her for consideration, but time was almost up. He'd give her another twenty-four hours, but if there was no word, he planned to make good on his promise to contact her.

"You're a good man, Linc."

"Don't tell anyone. No one would believe you but it could be bad for my business reputation if that rumor got out."

"There's this handy thing called attorney-client privilege and it means I'm not allowed to reveal your confidential information."

Even if Mason swore on a bible, Linc was pretty sure Rose wouldn't believe him. Leaving her had ripped out his heart and if she hurt even half that bad it made what he'd done unforgivable. So, the longer it took for her to get back to him, the more determined he became to hire her. If necessary he would sweeten the deal. Somehow...

His cell phone rang and he picked it up, checking the caller ID. What a coincidence. Before it sounded again, he answered. "Rose."

"Hello, Linc. I've been thinking about what you said."

Her voice was businesslike with just a hint of sultriness in the slight lisp. It took a lot of self-control to hold off on a hard sell. "And?"

"I'd like to discuss it in more detail."

"Okay. I'll meet you for dinner. In say..." He looked at the watch on his wrist. "An hour?"

"Tonight?" She sounded surprised.

"Yes. I'm free." He met Mason's gaze and shrugged.

"Tomorrow at my studio would be fine," she said.

Did she have a date? With the guy she was "almost engaged" to? A knot tightened in his gut. "Do you have plans?"

"No, but—"

"Then I'll pick you up in about an hour," he said. "What do you say?"

There was hesitation on the other end of the line that was just about to turn awkward. Then she said, "I'll meet you at the diner. There's only one in Prosper so you can't miss it."

"Okay. See you then."

After he ended the call Mason cleared his throat. "So, I get bumped for dinner with your wife. Should my feelings be hurt?"

"Come on, Mason. We both know lawyers don't have feelings." He grinned at the other man. "You said yourself this was a smart move. I have to close the deal on my goodwill gesture."

And if this was a little more than goodwill that would just be a secret not even his attorney knew.

Rose didn't know what to make of the fact that Linc was able and, dare she say it, eager to have this meeting on such short notice. She hesitated to say he dropped everything but it kind of felt that way.

She'd intended to be at the diner first but got a call about a potential job and had to take it. She wanted to be the one watching him make the long walk past the counter and swivel stools to the booths and tables at the far end. In a perfect world they would both have arrived at the same time, but why should her world start being perfect now? A world where she was in control and not nervous about what the man who'd walked out on her was up to.

Now she was late and moving toward a table in the back, where he was sitting and staring at *her*.

If only she knew what he was thinking. On the upside… She was ten years older and less likely to give a rat's behind what Lincoln Hart was thinking. It had taken her a long time to get to a place where she didn't care and no matter what Vicki thought, she really didn't.

She slid into the red-padded booth seat and met his gaze across the gray Formica table. "Sorry I'm late."

"No problem." There was a nearly empty coffee mug in front of him. Apparently he'd been here long enough to drink it.

Rose waited to feel guilty about keeping him waiting, but couldn't quite manage. "I had to take a work call."

"Of course," he said reasonably. "I hope it wasn't a crisis situation."

As opposed to sitting across from the man who once broke her heart and trying to pretend that same heart wasn't pounding so hard it might give out?

She shook her head. "No crisis."

"Good."

Again she cursed the unfairness of him looking even better than he had ten years ago. She didn't remember his eyes being such a dark shade of blue or that his shoulders were quite so wide. Could be the white dress shirt he was wearing, with the long sleeves rolled up to midforearm. It was a look she'd once loved on him and that thought didn't do much to slow her pulse.

"So I'm glad you called," he said.

"Hmm?" She blinked, suddenly realizing she'd been staring at his chest while her mind skipped down memory lane, very close to the point where she wondered how he looked without a shirt now. "Right. My call. Thanks for meeting me."

"You wanted to discuss the job offer."

"Yes."

Before she could say more, the waitress came over to take their orders. Rose had been hungry until seeing Linc put knots in her stomach the size of a Toyota. But she figured a half-sandwich-and-salad combo would work. He asked for a burger and fries so obviously his appetite was totally unaffected by seeing her. That was irritating.

When they were alone again she asked, "Where is this condo again? The one you need decorated?"

"Blackwater Lake, Montana. It's a picturesque town that's being compared to Vail and Aspen in Colorado."

"And what are we talking about? Paint? Furniture? A theme?"

He nodded. "Everything. Flooring, fixtures, carpet. Right now it's just a shell and the builder left it that way at my request."

"It's my understanding that you can't get a mortgage unless the flooring is installed."

"I don't have a mortgage."

Of course he didn't. His family had buckets of money. Whether or not he was a Hart by blood, clearly Linc was one of their own. Rose refused to wonder what it would have been like to be married to him and not have to worry about the money to pay her rent. It would be dishonest to say she hadn't been dazzled by the glitz and glamour of the Hart name and all it represented, but that's not why she'd fallen in love with him.

"So you're talking about cupboards, sinks and everything?"

"Yes."

"Then you're not living there yet."

"No," he replied.

Rose waited for him to fill in the blank of where he *did* stay but that didn't happen. "Are there accommodations in this picturesque place?"

"I'll handle that and pay all of your expenses."

There was a question she just had to ask because it would be stupid not to. "What's in this for you, Linc?"

His easygoing expression didn't waver. "I get a beautifully decorated condo. What else would there be?"

"That's what I'd like to know. You led me on once and

even married me to get what you wanted, so I'd just like to know if I should be worried."

"I can't stop you. But I give you my word that I only want to take advantage of your decorating expertise to make my place a serene and comfortable space to live in."

"So this time you're not planning to get me into bed and have your way with me under false pretenses?"

His gaze narrowed, a sign that the barb drew a little blood. "There were no false pretenses the first time."

"I don't believe you."

"There's nothing I can say to change that." His mouth pulled tight for a moment. "But let me add this—I researched your company and it's in trouble. Decorating my place is more than a job. It's an opportunity for the kind of publicity that you can't afford. I feel badly about what happened and this is my way of making it up to you."

So it was pity.

The words made her feel both better and worse. There was some satisfaction in calling him on the crap he'd pulled but he really had all the power. Her business needed help and no one else was offering. "Okay, then. I'll put together a contract with a rough estimate of my time and a price. You can decide if it's acceptable."

"It will be."

"You haven't seen anything yet."

"I don't have to." He took a sip of coffee and met her gaze over the rim of the mug.

She knew he was a successful executive and didn't achieve his level of affluence by making bad deals. "What if the charges are inflated?"

"I have trust."

"That makes one of us because I don't trust you."

"You've made that really clear. And I completely understand." Again with the irritating reasonableness. "I'm happy to pay whatever you want to charge for your services."

"You do realize I'm not a hooker."

Even though it had been a quickie marriage in Vegas that's the way he'd made her feel ten years ago. Her words produced barely a flicker of an eyelash but she knew they'd hit their target again. Well, too darn bad. And the exhilaration she felt right now was proof that she'd deliberately provoked him. Not smart to cut off her nose to spite her face but she just couldn't help it. That's not something she would have said to any other client and she had better try to rein in the sarcasm because there was no telling how far he could be pushed. "I'll rephrase," he said. "Whatever your interior-designer fee is I will pay it, along with travel and living expenses while we are in Blackwater Lake."

"You're going, too? It can all be done in email—"

"I have business there anyway."

Of course she'd suspected he probably would be going but when he put the words out there the reality of it all really sank in. If she was going to back out it would have to be now.

Control was an illusion because she really had little choice. No way her business was going down without a fight. She met his gaze. "Agreed."

"Excellent." He looked decidedly pleased and that was irksome.

Which was why she added, "I'm glad you decided to have this meeting in person. I felt it necessary to emphasize how much I don't trust you and wanted to see your reaction to my terms."

"And?"

"You fooled me once, but this time I'm in the driver's seat." Although it was kind of a pathetic seat since she had very little bargaining room.

The waitress returned with a tray bearing food and she set plates in front of them. "Can I get you anything else?"

"Ketchup," she and Linc said together.

"You know each other pretty well." The woman smiled and pointed to the condiments next to the napkin dispenser. "It's already on the table."

Linc met her gaze when they were alone. "So, you haven't forgotten that I like ketchup with fries."

"If memory serves it was practically a religious experience," she said.

"Yeah. Nice to know some things don't change."

And some do when the man you'd loved with every fiber of your being treated you like a mistake. Anger flared again but she willed it away. Losing control with Lincoln Hart was not an option. "Where does the divorce stand?"

"My attorney is working on it."

"Are you paying full price this time?" Darn. The sarcasm just popped out of her mouth. Apparently he didn't bring out the best in her.

But Linc smiled. "With what I'm paying Mason he could put a child through college and multiple postgraduate degrees as well as buy several vacation homes and probably a boat."

"Does Mason have a child?"

"He's not married. And before you remind me that vows aren't necessary to produce a child, I'll just say no. He doesn't have any kids."

"So one can assume that the dissolution of our marriage is progressing at an appropriately acceptable pace?"

"It is." He took a bite of his hamburger and chewed. After swallowing he said, "Is there some reason you want to accelerate the process?"

"Nothing has changed since we last spoke." She pushed

lettuce around her plate without eating any. "I just don't like loose ends."

He set down his burger and wiped his hands on a napkin before pulling a business card from his wallet. He set it on the table and slid it over to her. "This is my lawyer's contact information. Feel free to get in touch with him anytime and ask anything you want. Or have your attorney get in touch with him."

"Okay." She picked up the card and put it in her purse and made a mental note to pass it along to Vicki. "As long as everything goes smoothly I'll be happy."

"How do you define a not-smooth divorce?"

"You disappearing without explanation would put a speed bump in the divorce road." This saying the first thing that popped into her head was becoming a bad habit that only seemed to happen with Linc.

"Don't worry. I'll be around until the papers come."

That would be an improvement over last time, but doing better than he had ten years ago wasn't setting a very high bar.

In the meantime she had a job. That was the good news. Unfortunately she would be working for the man she was just a little bit married to. Did that make her nervous?

Did beavers build dams?

Chapter Three

"So your dad wasn't using the private plane today?"

Linc stared at Rose, sitting across from him in the cushy leather airplane seat. They'd taken off and reached cruising altitude, and there was a steady hum in the pressurized cabin of the Gulfstream jet. They were on their way to Blackwater Lake and hiring a jet for transportation was the most efficient way to get there. Comfort didn't hurt, either. And there might be a little bit of trying to impress her going on.

"If you're talking about Hastings Hart, he's not my father. This aircraft doesn't belong to his company. And you should let it go. I have."

"Really? It doesn't feel that way to me." She tapped a finger against her lips. "Is the jet yours?"

"Not yet." It would be soon. But her comment had him curious. "In what way do you think I haven't let the paternity thing go?"

"You're awfully defensive. You were a grown man when you found out the truth and never suspected before that, which means you were loved and there's a bond. That doesn't just go away."

"You don't understand."

"Right. My bad."

Hell, how could she understand? He didn't, and it had happened to him. But his defensive response only served to sharpen the wary look in her eyes that never disappeared. It was as if any second she expected him to jump out of the plane and skydive so he could be anywhere but here.

It was on the tip of his tongue to say he'd left for her and she didn't understand, but that retort didn't work a moment ago and wouldn't now. "I don't remember you being this annoying."

"Probably because I wasn't," she said cheerfully. "We were firmly in the adoration stage of the relationship. And your abrupt departure didn't give me a chance to trot out the real me."

"Well, this is going to be fun. A guilt trip from Texas to Montana." They'd settled on her giving him four weeks to get the job going, then periodic trips back when necessary. So, for the next month he was going to let her say whatever she wanted to get off her chest. Redemption wasn't going to come without a price, he reminded himself.

"Suck it up, Linc. My attitude has been ten years in the making."

It was going to be a long flight if he didn't get her off this. And he had just the thing to ask. "What does your boyfriend think about you flying off with your husband for a job?"

Her smug expression slipped and she had no stinging comeback, which was a big clue that there was a ripple in the relationship pond.

"Rose?"

"What?"

"Did you tell—" He stopped. If she'd told him the guy's name he couldn't remember?

"Chandler," she said.

"You did tell Chandler about this job in Montana, right?"

She looked out the airplane window and shifted in her seat before meeting his gaze. "Yes, but before you ask, I didn't tell him about our past."

"Practically engaged and keeping secrets already? Tsk."

"Don't judge. You don't know me."

He'd known her once and she was an open book. Sweet and innocent. Generous and loving. There'd been no cynicism in her then and the fact that she had it now was another black mark on his soul. Another sin to lay at his feet.

However, he couldn't deny that the idea of trouble in paradise was damned appealing. "Should I read anything into the fact that you kept the details of our venture to yourself?"

"You can jump to any conclusions you want. I can't stop you and you're quite good at it." Her look challenged him to deny the statement.

Okay. Battle lines drawn. She was on the offensive so that's where he'd go, too. "What exactly did you tell him? You must have said something. He's bound to notice that you're not around. I certainly would if you and I were involved."

Every day for the last ten years he'd noticed that she wasn't there.

"I told him that I was going to be very busy."

He couldn't tell whether it was guilt or defiance in her tone. A little more pushing couldn't hurt because he'd already damaged her and he had little left to lose. "Too busy to see him?"

"Yes."

"And he's okay with that?"

"I'm so lucky. Chandler is a sweet, understanding man. He's supportive of my career."

"A real saint."

He knew couples made compromises. His mother and Hastings compromised the truth about Linc for their relationship. But unquestioningly letting the woman you loved fly to Montana with another man, even one she was divorcing, seemed wrong to him.

Come to think of it there was something else he wanted to know. "Is Chandler aware that you're a married woman?"

"Oh, please. I'm not—"

"Don't deny it. We've already gone over this. There's no divorce, so technically we are still married." He folded his arms over his chest and couldn't quite keep the "gotcha" out of his voice. "You didn't tell him."

"I don't remember you being this annoying, either." She stared at him and must have realized he wasn't backing down because there was a lot of resignation in her sigh. "No. I never told him about the marriage."

Why? he wanted to ask. Was she afraid that would destroy their relationship? A man who truly loved her wouldn't give a tinker's damn about this. Linc remembered how it felt to love her. In the same situation, if she'd dropped this bombshell on him, he'd have hired the best divorce attorney on the planet to dissolve the union so he could marry her. Making her his was more important than anything. Correction: it would have been, if he was Chandler.

"On the upside," he said cheerfully, "since he doesn't

know about the marriage it saves you the trouble of having to break the news that you're not divorced."

She huffed out a breath. "Not only are you annoying, you're a smart-ass."

"Is that any way to talk to the man who's funneling work your way?"

"We both know you're not the typical client. Other than my expertise on decorating you have an agenda. I haven't figured out what it is yet but we both know there is one."

"You're even more creative than I knew." He knew how smart she was and shouldn't have been surprised she'd guessed. "I look forward to seeing what you come up with for my condo."

"Do you take anything seriously?"

"Of course."

"Like what?" she demanded.

"My business."

"That's not what I meant and you know it. What about your family?" There was a gleam in her eyes now. "Come to think of it, I have no idea what you've been up to and you know an awful lot about me."

"Because you've been very generous in sharing details."

"My mistake," she said. "Let's even the playing field. Tell me about your personal relationship."

"What makes you think I have one?"

She gave him an "oh, come on" look. "I guess a specific question would be better. And before you give me an evasive answer, consider that there's still a lot of flight time left and I can be persistent."

"Okay, I've been warned. What would you like to know?"

She gave him a thoughtful look for several moments. "Since you left me, have you been close to needing a marriage license?"

"Since you, marriage has not once entered my mind."

He'd never let a woman that close because it wasn't fair to lead anyone on. Marriage wasn't a step he would ever take again.

"Hmm. That brings up more questions than it answers." Rose tucked a long strand of shiny dark hair behind her ear as she studied him. "Is that because of what happened with your parents?"

"Hastings isn't my father."

"He still parented you with your mother. Is it that? Or was marriage to me so bad? Did I break you, Linc?"

Leaving her did, but that wasn't her fault. It was the only way he could think of to protect her from the mess that was his life. Eventually he had put the pieces back together and if they didn't quite fit, that wasn't on her.

"You know better than anyone, Rose, that I'm a bad risk."

"At least you're taking responsibility." There was a flash of what looked like sympathy on her face before she shut it down. "But ten years is a long time. I don't quite know what to make of the fact that you're alone."

"Let's just call it a public service." When she opened her mouth to protest, he said, "Want a drink? The bar is stocked. Let's go check out the galley and see what we can find."

"Don't think I didn't see how you just tried to distract me from your love life. And I'll admit it worked, but only because I've never been on a private plane before."

"I'd never have guessed, what with your cool, sophisticated demeanor."

"Don't let that fool you. On the inside I'm giddy with curiosity and excitement."

Until this moment Linc hadn't realized how much he'd missed teasing her. And her honesty. He didn't know any woman who wouldn't have pretended that a lift on anything but a commercial flight happened every day. Her excitement at a new experience was charming and brought back memories of his eagerness to introduce her to all the pleasures life had to offer.

Including sex.

He'd given up the right to her body and the tempting curves in front of him now. Settling for drinks and hors d'oeuvres on a jet paled in comparison but that was all he could hope for. And the remainder of the flight passed quickly with a bottle of wine and snacks that had Rose moaning in ecstasy while he questioned how much pain he could handle on the road to redemption.

The Gulfstream landed at the recently opened Blackwater Lake Airport. A Mercedes SUV was waiting and he stowed their luggage while Rose let herself into the passenger seat. He got behind the wheel and drove into town, pointing out the highlights along the way.

"This is a very small place," she commented, sounding less than thrilled.

"You're observant. I always said that about you."

"Oh—" She pointed out the window. "The Blackwater Lake Lodge. That's the first hotel I've seen. It looks nice."

He drove past and left the city limits. "Right now it's the only hotel in town."

She glanced over her shoulder. "Then why didn't you stop?"

"Because we're not staying there."

"Linc—" There was warning in her voice. "This is where we talk about how much I don't like surprises. You promised that you'd handle accommodations."

"And I have."

"If you're planning to pitch a tent and expect me to

camp out, it would be best if you turned around and put me on the first plane back to Texas."

"Where we're going there are great views and a lot of square footage."

"Wilderness doesn't count. Somewhere in this town there must be a roof and indoor plumbing," she warned.

"There is. Trust me."

"I thought we were clear that I don't trust you."

He was going to do his damnedest to change her mind about that.

Rose was uneasy after Linc bypassed the Blackwater Lake Lodge and kept driving. Finally he turned right and pulled into a long driveway leading to a big house at the top of a rise. The sun was just going down behind the majestic mountains, but there was still enough light to see that the grounds were stunning. A carpet of perfectly manicured green grass was surrounded by flowers and shrubs.

He stopped the SUV by a brick walkway leading to gorgeous double front doors with oval glass insets. "I think this will fit your definition. There's a roof and indoor plumbing. The rest of it isn't bad, either."

"This can't be your place because you said it's a condo and currently unlivable." She left her seat belt buckled. "What's going on? You said you'd handle expenses and accommodations but—"

"This is my sister's place. She lives here with her husband and daughter."

"Why?"

"Because they're married and need a place to raise their child." His tone was wry.

"No. Why aren't we at a hotel?"

"As we established there's only one in town and I

couldn't get a reservation. Late spring is nice here in the mountains and it's becoming a popular tourist destination."

Rose studied him. He was looking awfully darn pleased with himself, but it felt like he'd pulled one over on her and she didn't like it a bit. "I don't know what you're up to, but—"

"And here's my sister now." He pointed to the open front door.

Rose saw a little girl run outside, followed immediately by a man and woman. Linc exited the car and came around to her side to open the door. His family didn't look intimidating but what did she know? These people were related to him.

Rose got out and muttered under her breath, "You should have warned me about this."

"If I did, would you have taken the job?"

That was a good question. Probably she would have but he hadn't given her the chance to decide. Again.

"Linc!" His sister threw herself into his arms.

He grabbed her and lifted her off the ground in a big hug. "Hey, baby sister. You look good."

"You, too." Then she smiled at Rose. "Hi. I'm Ellie McKnight."

"Rose Tucker." She shook the woman's hand as the two men greeted each other.

"This is her husband, Alex, and this munchkin is their daughter, Leah."

"Nice to meet you." Rose smiled at the little girl observing the hectic scene from the safety of her handsome father's strong arms. "She's beautiful."

"Just like her mom," Alex said proudly.

Ellie took the child and said, "Honey, why don't you help Linc bring their bags inside."

"Right."

"Rose, welcome to our home."

"Thank you. I appreciate your hospitality, but if it's too much of an inconvenience I can find something—"

"Absolutely not. It's been too long since I had a good visit with my brother. We're happy to have you and I'm glad you agreed to stay with us."

It would probably be rude to say she hadn't agreed to anything because he hadn't shared the trip details with her. So, she kept that to herself. Linc, however, was going to get an earful.

Ellie led her past the living and dining rooms into the huge kitchen–family room combination. There was a river-rock fireplace on one wall with a big flat-screen TV above. Leather sofas and cloth-covered chairs formed a conversation area in front of it and the thick, neutral-colored carpet was littered with pink toys and dolls. When her mom set her down, Leah plopped herself in the middle of it and started playing.

Moments later the men joined them and Alex informed his wife, "Bags are by the stairway. I wasn't sure where you wanted everyone."

"Thanks, honey. I think Linc and Rose might want to catch their breath."

Rose doubted that would happen, at least for her. Since the moment Linc had showed up in her life again she felt as if she'd had the air knocked out of her. Then on the plane he'd confessed that after her he'd never again considered marriage. What did that mean? Had it been awful with her? Resentment pointed her in that direction, but when he'd said it there was a wistful, sad look on his face. And now he'd brought her to stay with his sister. This must be how Dorothy felt when the tornado dropped her in Oz. Rose was definitely not in Texas anymore.

"Can I get you something to drink? Are you hungry?"

Ellie asked. "I've got some appetizers to put out and we'll have dinner in a little while."

"I hope you haven't gone to any trouble," Rose protested.

The other woman waved away her concern. "It's cheese and crackers and Alex is going to grill. Very easy."

Linc looked at her. "How about a glass of wine?"

"That would be nice. White?"

"Done," Ellie said. "And Linc will want a beer."

"I'll take care of the drinks, sweetie," her husband offered.

Rose stood beside Linc on the other side of the huge kitchen island and watched the attractive couple work together. A smile here, a touch there. A closeness and intimacy she'd never had the chance to form with Linc. Envy and regret mixed with her lingering anger at what he'd done to *them*.

When everyone had drinks Ellie held up her wineglass and said, "Let's drink to me."

Linc grinned and said, "Now why would we do that?"

"Because I talked you into moving to Blackwater Lake, which makes me pretty awesome. You're going to thank me for this."

Alex touched his longneck beer bottle to his wife's glass. "I thought you were awesome even before your brother bought his condo. And I thank my lucky stars every day that you came into my life."

Rose wanted to hold on to her envy and dislike of these two, but she was powerless. They were so cute, so friendly. She tapped her glass to theirs. "I think you're awesome for wanting to put up with your brother as a full-time resident."

There was a funny look on Linc's face when he joined the toast. "To my favorite sister."

"I'm your only sister."

"I knew there was a reason you had to be my favorite because you're a pain in the neck."

"Takes one to know one," Rose said, meeting his gaze as she took a sip of her wine.

"I like her," Ellie said enthusiastically to the two men. "Linc told me you're friends. How did you meet?"

"At work," Linc said, jumping right in.

It took Rose a couple of beats to realize Ellie was clueless about their relationship, the fact that they were married and Linc had left her. Women had a way of picking up details, especially personal ones, so if his sister was clueless it was a good bet that the rest of his family was, too.

"Did you decorate Linc's offices in Dallas?" Ellie persisted.

"No," Linc answered for her again.

Rose didn't miss the fact that he looked more than a little uncomfortable about the turn this conversation was taking. Apparently when he was handling accommodations he hadn't factored in the part where his sister would be curious about them. It wasn't often that someone got what was coming to them so quickly or that the wronged party was around to see. He was getting what he deserved and she was a witness, so karma would have to forgive her for gloating.

She was waiting for more questions, but Leah chose that moment to toddle over and grab her mother's jeans-clad leg. She started to whine and, when picked up, pointed to the crackers-and-cheese plate on the island.

"Someone's hungry," Ellie said, quickly kissing the rosy-cheeked little girl before handing her to her father. "I don't want her to fill up on snacks. Honey, if you could put her in the high chair and feed her that would help. It would be better if she eats before we do."

"Gotcha, little bit," he said, tickling his daughter to make her giggle.

"While you do that, I'll show Linc and Rose to the guest wing so they can freshen up."

The three of them grabbed the bags and took them upstairs, following Ellie to the end of the long hall.

"So, it's a guest wing," Linc said. "Aren't you the grand one?"

"No. Just awesome." Ellie grinned at him, then pointed out the two large bedrooms connected by a bathroom. "Rose, I'm putting you in the one with the window seat that faces the backyard and mountains. Dallas is flat and I thought you might enjoy a different view. Linc, you take the other one." A piercing wail came from downstairs. "I'd better go help Alex. Hungry and tired is not an attractive combination on my daughter. See you two in a few."

Alone in the hall Rose met Linc's gaze. "So, your sister doesn't know we were married."

"No."

"You kept me a secret—"

"No." He took her arm and tugged her into his bedroom, then shut the door. "Not a secret."

"When you withhold significant life details from your favorite sister it kind of falls under the heading of secret."

"That was a complicated time." He didn't look happy.

Tough, she thought. "You were ashamed of me."

"No." His voice was sharp. "Not you. It was all me. My bad. Then I took a long break from everyone and everything. After that there was no point in saying anything."

"So now we're in Blackwater Lake and staying with your sister. Arrangements that you made and didn't see fit to share with me."

"Look, I know you're miffed—"

"That's way too nice a word for what I'm feeling," she snapped. "But there's a silver lining."

"What's that?" There was a wary look in his eyes.

"You didn't think it through about how to explain me."

He nodded grimly. "I thought you were enjoying that a little too much."

"Actions have consequences—even after ten years. Especially if you keep secrets."

"Look, Rose, I was a jerk."

"Was?" She folded her arms over her chest.

"I apologized for it and I'm handling the divorce," he continued, ignoring the dig. "I groveled."

"Yes, you did." She would give him that.

"Ellie and I are close. She's the one who convinced me to come back after I left—"

"And you don't want your favorite sister to know how big a jackass you are," she mused.

"I'm not comfortable with the jackass part," he said, "but essentially you're right. I'd consider it a big favor if you would keep the details of our relationship just between us."

Rose was loving this. Confident and unflappable Lincoln Hart was insecure and uneasy. "You know, this is a very unfortunate time for you to find out that what they say about reaping what you sow is true."

"Could you be a little more specific?" Tension tightened his jaw.

"I don't trust you," she reminded him.

"So you're going to rat me out to my sister?"

Rose shrugged, then walked through the connecting bathroom and closed the door behind her. This was too sweet. She was charging him an arm and a leg for this decorating job, which was pretty great all by itself. But now she had leverage and that was priceless.

Chapter Four

The morning after their arrival at his sister's, Linc waited a decent length of time for a sign that Rose was finished in the bathroom they shared. He'd been a gentleman; ladies first. But the longer it went on the more certain he was that this was revenge.

He knocked lightly on the door. "Are you going to be finished in there sometime in the next millennium?"

"Come in," she answered sweetly.

He did and there she was, putting on makeup and wearing nothing but a satiny pink robe that tied at her small waist and outlined her breasts. For several moments staring was his only option because he was pretty sure he'd swallowed his tongue. Her legs were smooth and tanned. He knew that because a lot of leg was showing due to the fact that the robe stopped way above her knees. Her feet were bare and the pink-polished toes did things to his insides that had never been done before.

Without looking away from the mirror Rose said, "One would think you'd never seen me put on makeup before and we both know you have."

It was true. He had seen her do this ordinary thing that women do, but now this was so much more intense and he wasn't sure why. Rather than directly address her comment he said, "I didn't know you were such a bathroom hog."

"You didn't stick around long enough to find out anything about me. Lucky you. Maybe you dodged a bullet."

He settled a shoulder against the doorjamb. "Putting a finer point on the situation, I didn't dodge you. We're still married."

"Only on paper."

Meaning there was no hanky-panky of the physical kind going on. But looking at her now, leaning forward to brush mascara on her long, thick lashes and watching the way her breasts strained against that pink satin material made him want to scoop her up, carry her to the bed and engage in hanky-panky for a week.

If he didn't know how soft her skin was, how it smelled and tasted, the temptation might have been easy to ignore. But he did know. He'd never forgotten and more than once since leaving her he'd nearly caved, every time barely stopping himself from begging her to take him back.

The same thing that stopped him then stopped him now. Protecting her from the Hart bastard was the most important thing, along with the overriding conviction that dragging her into his mess was wrong. On top of that, considering she thought he was maybe one life form above pond scum, any move he made on her would likely get his face slapped.

And he wouldn't lift a hand to stop her.

She glanced at him. "I can finish up in my room if you have to—"

"You're fine. All your stuff is here." He looked at the collection of brushes, containers, tubes and bottles. "And it's quite an impressive amount of stuff."

"A girl needs every advantage."

"Not you. Your face is naturally beautiful already."

She looked at him and there was a frown in her eyes. "I wasn't fishing for compliments and you don't have to hand them out. Our divorce is on track. Contracts have been signed guaranteeing my lucrative consultation fee on your condo. There's no reason for you to butter me up."

"I wasn't doing that." And he hadn't meant to say it. The words just came out of his mouth because he forgot for a split second all the crap that had happened, that they were no longer newlyweds who were crazy in love. "It was just my honest opinion."

She faced him and put a hand on her hip, the posture a sign that she was still peeved about something. "That's not fair."

"Since my observation was completely sincere I have no clue what the problem is."

"You didn't give me anything for a comeback. How can I say don't be honest or that I don't trust you? Especially when you're saying something nice to me?"

"You have no frame of reference to believe this, but I am a nice man."

"You're right," she agreed.

That was a surprise. "You think I'm nice?"

"No. I have no frame of reference to accept your words as fact." She turned back to the mirror and assessed her appearance before nodding with satisfaction. "The bathroom is all yours. I've done the best I can do with my face."

Her best was pretty damn good.

When he was alone Linc blew out a long breath and knew his shower was going to be colder than usual, courtesy of Miss Rose Tucker. Although technically she was Mrs. Lincoln Hart. They were married and he wanted her possibly even more than he had before whisking her to Las Vegas for a wedding. But she was forbidden fruit and being this close without being able to touch her was his hell to pay.

It didn't take Linc long to clean up and as he started downstairs he hoped to beat Rose. What with seeing her practically naked, he'd forgotten that she hadn't promised to keep their marriage a secret from his sister. The less time Rose and Ellie had alone to talk, the better. Then he heard the female voices coming from the kitchen and realized she dressed faster than she did hair and makeup. There was enough going on right now without his baby sister finding out about his screwup.

Ellie had always looked up to him and more than once called him her hero. When his life had turned upside down she'd been his anchor and he'd been extraordinarily grateful that at least one thing hadn't changed. He wanted to keep it that way.

He walked into the kitchen. "Good morning, ladies."

"Hey, slowpoke," Ellie said. "Hope you slept well."

"Great," he lied. There'd been no restful slumber with only a bathroom separating his room from Rose's. "So you two are all chummy this morning. What have you been talking about?"

"This and that." Rose was standing next to Ellie on the other side of the island with a knife in her hand. There was a pile of sliced mushrooms in front of her. "Girl stuff."

Best not to push that subject. "Speaking of girls, where is my niece?"

"With her father. Alex took her into town for breakfast." Ellie poured coffee into a mug and handed it to him.

"Thanks," he said, then picked up the subject of his

brother-in-law. "Doesn't he have a job to go to? It was my understanding that his construction company had more work than he could handle and that's why he and I are going to be partners."

"He's going into the office a little late. He does that once or twice a week, if possible. Daddy-daughter bonding. He calls it his Leah time."

"Aww, that's so sweet," Rose said. "He's really setting a high bar for dads."

"Every girl should have that." Ellie nodded emphatically.

Linc knew Rose had been raised by a single mom and recognized the wistfulness in her expression.

His sister must have seen it, too, because she said, "What was your father like, Rose?"

"That's a good question," she said. Her tone was indifferent. "My mom told him she was pregnant and he was never seen or heard from again."

"Jerk. And it's his loss," Ellie said.

"You can't miss what you never had," Rose commented philosophically.

"In the spirit of full disclosure, I was pregnant before Alex and I got married. Now this is girl talk," Ellie warned him. "We hadn't known each other very long but things got complicated pretty quickly. I was so in love and didn't think he cared. When Linc called to check up on me, which he always does, I told him everything and he was here the next day."

"Wow." Rose gave him a "who would have thought that of you?" look. "A sensitive side."

"Not when he punched Alex." His sister slid him a rueful look. "He was sure I'd been taken advantage of."

Rose shot him a skeptical look. "A regular Rocky."

"You had to be there," he said.

"It was actually very sweet once all the testosterone returned to normal levels. In the end everything worked out and Alex and I couldn't be happier." She smiled at Linc. "And now you're going to be living here in Blackwater Lake. I'm going to love having you around. So, you'd better be okay with Alex making time in his schedule for his daughter if you're going to partner up with him."

"Of course I am. Why would you even think I wouldn't be?" Linc asked.

"Good question. You and Rose are friends so she probably has a better answer than me. Or at least a theory."

Linc looked at the woman in jeans and pink sweater, unable to shake the image of her bare feet and polished toes. When had pink become such an erotic color? She met his gaze and there was a gleam in her eyes that made him nervous.

Rose cleared her throat. "The thing is, your brother hasn't had to think about anyone but himself for a long time."

"True. Very astute of you to pick up on that." Ellie tapped her lip thoughtfully as she studied him. "Linc, have you ever had to be unselfish and put someone else's needs before your own?"

"Of course I have."

"When?" Rose was clearly relishing her role in turning up the fire on his hot seat.

"Yeah, when?" Ellie asked.

"I have employees. A happy staff is an efficient staff. It's very basic."

"That's business," Rose pointed out.

"She's right, Linc. If you'd ever been in love, you would get what it means to put someone else first."

He got it big-time and had the dings in his heart as proof. But Rose didn't believe he'd put her well-being before his own and Ellie would be crushed and disappointed that he hadn't confided in her. He wasn't willing to lose what he had with his sister.

Since Ellie had made a statement instead of asking a question, Linc felt justified in not addressing her implication that he'd never been deeply in love. "Did anyone ever tell you that two against one isn't fair?"

"So, are you going to tattle on me to Dad?"

"Yours or mine?" The pity in his sister's eyes made him wish he could take back those words.

"Come on, Linc—"

"What? Get over it?" He sighed. "The fact is, Hastings is not my father. I've accepted that. There's no way to get over your DNA. It is what it is."

"But, still—"

"Ow." Rose dropped her knife.

"Did you cut yourself?" Linc was ready to jump in with first aid.

After checking her fingers for several moments she said, "No. Just a near miss."

"Thank goodness. Be careful. Those knives are really sharp." Ellie breathed a sigh of relief. "Okay, I think we have enough veggies. Let's get these omelets going." She went into command mode. "Rose, your help is much appreciated but I'll take it from here. Go have coffee with my brother."

"Yes, ma'am." Rose did as instructed and sat beside him at the island. There was a smug, satisfied expression on her face.

Suddenly Linc got it. His sister was banging pots and pans, so in a tone only Rose could hear he said, "You did that on purpose. Changed the subject."

"You're welcome." She blew on her coffee. "Even though you don't deserve it."

She'd proactively rescued him from his well-intentioned sibling. Would wonders never cease.

This redemption tour was not at all what he'd expected. One minute she was busting his chops, the next she had his back. He wasn't sure whether or not to be afraid of what she would do next.

"Thanks for getting Ellie off my back."

"Don't mention it. I gave you a distraction, you gave me a job. We're even."

"Not even close."

Rose was pretty sure he'd contracted her services to make things up to her, but didn't comment because a confirmation of her suspicions would make this a pity job.

They'd just left the house after breakfast and she sat in the passenger seat of the SUV while Linc drove to the condo. Pity or not she had work to do and wanted to see what she would be dealing with. They'd arrived yesterday just before sundown and she couldn't really see much. Now the sun was shining, the sky was vivid blue and the scenery was stunning. If she'd been behind the wheel, concentrating on the road would have been a challenge.

"You were not wrong," she said.

Linc glanced over. "I like the sound of that. But what are we talking about?"

"It's beautiful here. The mountains from my room... Majestic, stately, lush, tree-covered." She shrugged. "There are no words to adequately describe this place. And the view of the lake from your sister's family room is breathtaking."

He took his eyes off the road for a moment to look at her but aviator sunglasses hid his expression—although he was smiling. "I'm glad you like it."

Rose knew that smile, the one that used to turn her inside out and, unfortunately, still did a little. "I really do."

"Does that mean you trust me now?"

"Seriously? That was observation and opinion, not the basis on which to determine trustworthiness."

"Oh." He lifted one broad shoulder in a shrug. "A guy can hope."

Why in the world would he care? This was a job, not a relationship, and they were getting a divorce. When it was all over, their paths were unlikely to cross again. That thought should have been comforting but it produced a twinge of something that felt a little like regret. She chose not to comment.

Very soon she spotted a complex of buildings and Linc drove up to the guard gate and stopped the car. He pressed the button and his window went down as the private security guy walked out of the small hut and over to them.

"Nice to see you, Mr. Hart."

"You too, Jeff." He angled his head toward her. "This is Rose Tucker."

Jeff leaned over far enough to get a good look at her. "A pleasure, Miss Tucker."

"Hi." She lifted her hand in a wave.

"Can you put her on my list of approved people? She's my decorator and will need access to my place."

"Sure thing, Mr. Hart. I'll take care of it."

"Thanks."

"You folks have a good day."

The gate swung open for them and Linc drove through. There was a lush, grassy area straight ahead that was landscaped with bushes and flowers blooming in shades of pink, yellow, purple and orange. A charming gazebo stood in the center of the park and ornate streetlights were placed at intervals around it.

"This is like being in a different world," she said. "It's peaceful and pretty and perfect."

"That's what I thought, too."

"Can you drive through the whole complex so I can get a feel for it? I want the interior and exterior of your home to flow seamlessly together. Does that make any sense?"

"Not to me, but that's why I hired you." He kept driving around the grassy area. "It's not very big but this is just the first phase. Each successive one will be separated by a landscaped greenbelt and during future construction the existing residents won't be inconvenienced."

"Smart," she agreed. "The debris in the building stage is an eyesore. And the rogue nails are not the least bit tire-friendly."

As he drove around, Linc pointed out the community pool and clubhouse, which had state-of-the-art exercise equipment and facilities for receptions. It was zoned for a golf course and other amenities. This development had *exclusive* written all over it and probably the monthly up-keep costs were a small fortune on top of the no-doubt impressive price tag on his condo.

He slowed and pushed the button on a controller attached to his sun visor. One of the doors on a three-car garage went up. "This is it."

Rose looked around as he pulled the car into the drive-way. "This is an end unit. Very private."

"That's one of the things that sold me. Common walls between units are kept to a minimum. Condo living with the feel of a single-family detached home. Come on. I'll show you around."

She'd seen the floor plan and already had some notes, but knew that the place was over five thousand square feet on three levels. From the garage they walked into the first one, which was a large room with French doors leading to the backyard.

"Media room," she said absently.

"That's what I thought, too."

He led her up the stairs to the main living area. The rooms were clearly defined: kitchen, living, family and dining rooms. A bedroom and bath down the hall would make a great guest suite. But there were no floor coverings or cabinets. Just a lot of open space with numerous ways to configure it. Upstairs he showed her the huge master suite, then led the way into a long, large room that would be perfect as a spacious home office. And three more bedrooms and baths.

When they came back downstairs she stood in the kitchen, studying the dining room. "Again you weren't wrong. This is just a shell. And no, I haven't changed my mind about trusting you."

"Bummer."

"Do you entertain a lot?"

"Some. I wouldn't say a lot. Why?" he asked.

"Because the alcove between the kitchen and dining room is a perfect place for a butler's pantry."

"And that's different from a regular pantry…how?"

"It's where you store china, crystal, silver. The things you'd need for dinner parties."

"Hmm." He slid his fingers into the pockets of his jeans and frowned.

"What's wrong?"

"I'd rather negotiate a real estate deal than have to handle cloth napkins and place settings."

"You can hire a caterer," she suggested.

"Maybe."

"Why maybe?"

"There isn't a caterer in Blackwater Lake." He thought

for a moment. "Although Lucy Bishop might consider giving it a whirl."

Rose felt another twinge but this time it had nothing to do with regret. The sensation veered more into jealousy territory. This wasn't the time and she was in no mood to think about what that meant. "Who is she?"

"There's a place in town called the Harvest Café. She's a co-owner and the chef. Food is good and she might be persuaded to handle a private function."

"Ah."

"What?" He slid his sunglasses to the top of his head and there was sharp curiosity in his eyes. As if he'd seen her jealousy.

"Nothing. I said 'ah'—it was an acknowledgment that I heard and assimilated the information you related."

"Yes, but the tone of that single-syllable acknowledgement was full of…something."

Had he always been so perceptive? Rose remembered a lot about being with him but not that. She'd been blinded by love in their short time together and thought he was perfect. Now she realized that was an unrealistic expectation. A by-product of being so young and idealistic.

But he was waiting for an answer. "It's just…" She looked around the large space that was going to be spectacular when she got through with it and felt sad. "We never even moved into our own place. We weren't together long enough to set up housekeeping."

His frown deepened. "Is that going to be a problem for you? During this job?"

"Absolutely not. I'm a professional."

"I don't know what else to say, Rose. I copped to being a jerk. I've told you how sorry I am. What more do you want from me?"

She met his gaze and could see his words for the sincere

apology they were. But she'd been so young and hopeful and what he did changed her forever. It had to be said. "I guess I want those ten years back."

"If I could give them back to you I would do it in a heartbeat." He blew out a long breath, but it did nothing to take the edge off his intensity. "If there was anything I could do—"

She'd never get a better opportunity to press her advantage. "There is one thing."

His gaze narrowed on her. "I'm not going to like this, am I?"

"Probably not."

"For the record, there won't be any gold tassels or tapestries. I'm not a 'tassels and tapestry' kind of guy."

"Deal." She laughed and realized that was something else that hadn't changed. Linc could always make her smile and feel better about whatever bad thing had happened to spoil her day. "I'm wondering about something."

"Okay." But he looked as if he was bracing for a punch.

"We've established that Ellie doesn't know about us. That we dated. Got married. Split up. Getting around to the divorce now. You two are obviously close, so why would you not tell her?"

"Are you sure I can't just eat quiche? Or agree to a small tapestry somewhere? Maybe open a vein and bleed a little? The carpet isn't in yet."

"You asked what you can do and this is it. I'm curious."

He settled his hands on his hips and stared at the bare floor for a moment. "After I found out about my father, I told you I was gone for two years."

"Where did you go?"

"Europe."

"What did you do?" Did he miss her the way she missed him? Hurt the way she had?

"I did odd jobs. Drank." He met her gaze. "Ellie was the one who got me to come back."

"Not your parents?"

"No." His mouth tightened into a hard line. Not a shred of forgiveness there.

"How did Ellie do it?"

"It wasn't anything she said. I just missed her. My brothers, too, but she's always the one who could get to me."

"I envy you having siblings. You're lucky. That wasn't in the cards for me. And I just don't understand why you didn't tell her about the marriage."

"After so long it didn't seem relevant. And like she said, she always looked up to me."

"Her hero."

"Yeah. I didn't want her to be disappointed in me. The way I handled it."

"Isn't it possible she would laugh and tell you what a doofus you are?"

"You obviously don't know my sister." One corner of his mouth quirked up.

"I like her. She's generous, down-to-earth, funny and she loves you. I think it would take more than finding out about our marriage for her to abandon you."

"You're just saying that because you're dying to tell her what happened."

"Are you kidding?" Rose wanted to say "duh." "Who wouldn't want to?"

"So, why didn't you tell all?" he asked.

She'd once dreamed of having a traditional family with Linc but that wasn't in the cards for her any more than having siblings. He'd had it all—a mother and father who loved him, a family—and distanced himself from all of it, and that made her wonder. She looked around this space he wanted her to decorate.

"This condo is fabulous and it's clear to see why you're attracted to it. So don't take it wrong what I'm about to ask and keep in mind that I don't need to love a space to do a good job."

"Okay. Where are you going with this?"

"You could have bought a house. That would give you a place to live and room to grow. For a family of your own. Why not go that route? You're a bachelor now but that could change."

The teasing look disappeared and he turned serious. "I deeply regret that you got caught up in my personal family problems. I thought I knew what love was before I found out my parents lied to me all my life."

What was he saying? "You don't believe in love now?"

"No, I don't."

"What about Ellie and Alex? They're in love."

"She's a Hart, I'm not," he said, as if that explained it all.

There were so many things she could say. Harts were not the only humans on the planet allowed to find love. He deserved it, too. Flair for the dramatic much? But all the teasing had gone out of him and he was dead serious about this.

"Okay, then," she said, and walked around to hide her reaction. It made absolutely no sense, but Rose felt as if Linc had just walked out on her a second time. "The architect did a good job with window placement and building orientation. Every one has a spectacular view of either the lake or the mountains."

"That was Ellie."

She met his gaze. "What?"

"My sister is the architect." The teasing expression was back in his eyes. "And don't think I didn't notice what you just did there."

"Where? What?" she asked.

"The way you sidestepped answering my question."

His revelation had pushed the conversation out of her mind and she had no clue what he was referring to. "You asked something?"

"I did." He settled his hands on his hips. "Why haven't you told my sister about us being married?"

This was much less complicated than talking about him refusing love. "I haven't said anything *yet* because it's just too good having something to hold over you."

"If I beat you to the big reveal there goes the advantage," he challenged.

She shrugged. "Either way I get to watch. So go ahead and call my bluff."

This was new, she thought. Being in control of anything where Lincoln Hart was concerned. Rose decided that she liked it very much.

Chapter Five

The next morning Linc stepped out of the shower, then heard the bathroom door open and quickly wrapped a towel around his waist. He watched a sleepy Rose walk in like a zombie and his gut tightened at the sight of her—hair tousled as if she'd just had sex. Her eyes were half-closed the way he remembered them in the throes of passion. She'd told him once that in the morning she barely functioned until after coffee. Apparently that was still true because she hadn't signaled any awareness of his presence yet or the fact that he was nearly naked.

From his perspective, he had the better view of nearly naked. She was wearing a see-throughish camisole top and matching shorts that left her legs mostly bare. He wished they were all bare, but that was a thought that needed to stop right there.

"Good morning."

His voice must have worked like a shot of adrenaline

to blast her out of the trance because her eyes went wide and she gasped. She grabbed the hand towel hanging next to the sink and held it over her breasts.

"Linc! What are you doing in here?"

Obviously the adrenaline hadn't activated all her brain cells yet. "We share a bathroom. Remember?"

The part of him throbbing insistently wished they could share something even more intimate than that. Not ever going to happen, though. Even if she forgave him, he wouldn't get married again and she wouldn't settle for less than that. She'd made it clear ten years ago and the expression in her eyes yesterday when he'd answered her question about why a condo and not a house told him her position hadn't changed. Then the pity for him rolled in and he couldn't stand it.

"Sharing," she said. "Right. I'm sorry for barging in."

"No. I'm sorry. Should have locked your side, but I didn't. Just in case you needed something…"

She cocked her thumb over her shoulder. "I'll just leave and give you your privacy."

When she looked this hot and sexy, privacy was highly overrated. "Don't leave on my account."

She swallowed once and seemed to be very deliberately concentrating on looking him in the eyes and nowhere else. Like his chest, for instance. "That's okay. I'm good. Take your time."

In the short span of their marriage they hadn't spent many mornings together. Maybe that's why the memories were so vivid, because there'd been no time to become complacent, take each other for granted. Linc would never forget her fascination with him shaving. She'd explained about being an only child raised by a single mom. It was an all-female environment. But that innocent remark had filled him with so many profound feelings. Her inexperience and growing up without a father to teach her about the world and keep her safe. At that moment he'd promised himself that he would always protect her.

Everything he'd done after that was to honor that vow.

"I'm just going to shave, then it's all yours." He soaped up his cheeks and jaw, then picked up his razor and started the process that had always seemed a little less tedious after Rose.

"Interesting." She was still standing there. Watching.

"What is?"

"You go for the clean-shaven look when the current style for men is scruff."

"I guess I'm a traditional guy." Who was having a hard time not slitting his throat or cutting off an ear with the sharp instrument in his hand. The sight of her holding that ridiculous towel to hide what he'd already seen was too adorable. And distracting. But he'd rather lose an ear than send her away. If it was good enough for van Gogh...

"But you're a traditional guy who has no intention of settling down. That implies you need an infinite supply of female companionship."

He waited for more but she didn't say anything. It seemed she wasn't fully awake yet and he wanted a finer point on the female companionship thing. "What does that mean?"

"Women like a man with scruff. You need women. Therefore you should cultivate the scruff to attract them."

"Like bees?"

"To honey. Yes."

"And if I told you that the traditional look has been working just fine?" Would she be jealous?

She lifted one smooth, delicate shoulder in a shrug. "I'd say your women are uninspired."

Suddenly he was much less interested in women in

general than this one in particular. For just a moment he stopped shaving and met her gaze. "What inspires you?"

The pulse in her neck fluttered faster as she studied him. But when she answered, her voice was cool and even. "There's a lot to be said for a man with a smooth face…"

"But?"

"What?" she asked.

"You stopped. There was going to be more. There's something about a smooth face and I heard a 'but' in your voice. You were going to add…"

"It's not important."

"To me it is." He waited.

"Why?"

"That one little word could be a good or bad thing."

"Oh?"

"Think about it. A single-syllable word that leaves a clear path for a leap into a very bad place." He met her gaze while he thought about that. "Consider this. A smooth face is attractive on you *but* those features could stop a clock so maybe you should grow a beard."

She laughed. "I didn't mean that."

"Then what? You like smooth but if there was scruff on mine you'd be tempted to forgive and forget that I'm the jackass who left you?"

Her teasing smile slowly disappeared. "Look, Linc, I can't walk in your shoes. There's no way for me to understand what it feels like to find out what you did. No way that I can possibly get what you went through. Are still going through. And I won't patronize you by saying that I do. All I can tell you is that I believe you, that you had a reason for what you did." She shrugged as if to say sorry about this. "And that's the best I can do right now."

"Fair enough." He hadn't planned to ask forgiveness but didn't regret that he had. Her response was both less than he wanted and more than he deserved. For some stupid reason, and he did mean stupid, that gave him hope. For what, he didn't know. All he was sure of at this moment was how very much he wanted to kiss her and what a very bad idea it was.

"Let me know when you're finished in here." She started to turn away.

"Wait." He took the hand towel that was hanging beside the second sink and wiped all traces of soap from his face. "I need to talk to you in case I'm gone when you come down for breakfast."

"You're leaving early?"

"Alex and I have business to take care of. He wants me to see some property for development and look at office space for our company."

"When will you be back?"

"Not sure. I might be gone most of the day."

She nodded. "I've got work to do. Now that I've seen your place, I'll need to make sketches of each room and get some ideas put together for you. I do some on computer and others on paper."

"This house has more rooms than the entire von Trapp family could use. I'm sure Ellie can find space for you to work."

"Yeah. She already mentioned that to me and is going to help me set up somewhere."

"Good." That was his sister. Efficient and gracious. "And while I'm gone, don't say anything to her about our little secret."

There was a wicked look in her eyes. "I make no promises."

"You really are enjoying holding this over my head, aren't you?"

"So very, very much." She grinned.

They stared at each other for several moments and neither of them moved. But her smile faded and there was what looked like wistfulness in her eyes. Was it his imagination or wishful thinking that she was as reluctant and unwilling to lose this moment as he was?

So many thoughts flashed through his mind in those seconds. He'd never stopped wanting this woman and his need to kiss her right now bordered on desperate. She didn't hate him anymore, but did it matter since she was in a relationship that could be moving to the next level?

Except how did you take the next step after not telling your significant other you weren't free from a marriage he never knew about and were going to another state to work for your husband?

Linc had never been more painfully aware that she was his wife than right at this moment. But kissing her the way he wanted could destroy this fragile truce and any gains on having his sins forgiven. As much as he despised the thought of her with another man, sabotaging his opportunity to make things up to her wasn't something he was prepared to do.

"Okay, then," he said. "The bathroom is all yours."

Rose couldn't get the image of Linc shaving out of her mind. She was still thinking about it after showering, doing hair, makeup and walking downstairs. Was there anything sexier than a half-naked man dragging a straight-edge razor over his face? The bunch of muscles in his arm and the way his mouth twisted for the hard-to-get places. She hadn't been able to look away, which was something that hadn't changed in ten years.

Neither had her inability to function very well before coffee. She'd been like a sleepwalker, charging into the room and being only dimly aware of where she was and who she was charging in on. If he'd done that to her...

Well, she'd have to call it a lesson in tolerance and humility. Forgive and forget? Not if she was smart. Remembering and resentment were just about all that stood between her and being made a fool of again.

Ellie was the only one in the kitchen... Scratch that—the only adult. Leah toddled out from behind the island and grinned at her.

"Good morning." Rose smiled at the little girl. "Hey there, cutie."

"Did you sleep well?" Ellie asked.

"So good."

Ellie poured coffee into a mug, put in milk and a low-calorie sweetener and set it in front of her. "Linc told me how you take your coffee and said you really needed this."

"Thanks." Heat crept into her cheeks at the reminder of seeing him with just a towel knotted at his waist. She was still a little weak in the knees. "He said he and Alex had to leave early."

"Yeah. You just missed them." Ellie rested her elbows on the island between them, her gaze sharp and questioning. But all she said was "What would you like for breakfast?"

"Coffee is fine. Don't bother on my account."

"It's no trouble. And it's not all about you," the other woman teased. "The guys decided to grab something out so I waited to have a 'girls only' breakfast."

"That sounds wonderful. How can I help?"

"Set the table and keep an eye on Leah?" she asked.

"I can do that."

A short time later the little girl was in her high chair and the two women were eating scrambled eggs, toast and fruit.

Rose took a bite. "Mmm. These eggs are so light and fluffy. You'll have to tell me how to get them like this."

"Having someone watch my daughter so I don't burn them is the secret."

Rose took a bite of toast and sighed. "Why does everything taste so much better in the mountains?"

"No clue, but it's so true." The other woman cut fruit into tiny pieces and put them on the tray for her daughter. The little girl used her small fork to spear one, then maneuvered the food into her mouth. "Good job, baby girl."

As she ate Rose watched mother and child, envious of everything about them. If things had been different she and Linc might have kids now. Regret twisted inside her until she noticed Ellie watching her. The look wasn't quite suspicious, mostly speculation.

"I need to start working on designs for Linc's place. You said there's somewhere I can do that?"

"Yes. An office down the hall off the family room. Alex and I both use it but there's plenty of room and neither of us is in there during the day. After breakfast I'll get you settled."

"Thank you so much." She sincerely meant that.

Ellie put some eggs on her daughter's tray. "So, how long ago did you and Linc meet?"

"Oh…" She hesitated, trying to figure out what to say, then decided to stick to the truth. "Ten years, I think."

"That's a long time. I don't remember him ever mentioning you."

"He sure talked about you." Rose had always liked how much he cared about his sister. It spoke to the good man that he was and she hoped the pivot would take the focus off her and Linc. "He had a problem with your boyfriend at the time."

"He had a problem with *every* boyfriend I ever had. Including Alex, the love of my life. And now they're going to be business partners." Ellie's smile faded. "We talked about everything. Family. Friends. Linc never said anything about you, though. It just makes me wonder..."

Oh, boy. His sister didn't plan to let this go. "I suppose I should be hurt that I was so insignificant."

"That's the thing. I don't think you are."

Rose finished the last bite of food, then set her fork on the empty plate. "Why do you say that?"

"He knows how you take your coffee and was very specific with the details. Bordering on protective. That doesn't happen if a man is indifferent."

"When he told you he was bringing a decorator here, what did he say?"

"Not much," Ellie admitted. "And I didn't ask because I was so happy about him moving here."

"I know you're close." Rose got up and filled her mug with more coffee. She needed to think about what to say. "But why are you so excited about him moving here? Is it about missing family?"

"Some. But it's more than that. Linc went through a hard time finding out he had a different father." Her eyes widened, as if something just occurred to her. "That was ten years ago, in fact, right around the time you met him. So I'm sure he talked to you about it."

Not then, Rose thought. Still, she didn't want to add too many details. "He left and I missed him."

"My brother is so darn stubborn," Ellie said. "He won't speak to our parents about it and refuses to get to know his biological father. He cut the guy out of his life but doesn't get how that gives the man power over it."

Rose's eyes widened. "I never thought about it that way. If he'd only said something when he left—"

"Wait. Said something? If only... What?"

"Hmm?" *Crap and double crap*, Rose thought.

"Linc left you?"

"Did I just say that out loud?"

"Yes." Ellie was staring at her. "Look, something is up between you and my brother. I could see it from the first. And a little while ago when I told you he said you needed coffee, you were blushing."

"I was?"

"Trust me. The red was so bright it could be seen from space."

Rose blew out a long breath. "I guess my game face needs some work."

"If you're planning to hurt my brother, you'll have to go through me—"

"It's not like that, Ellie. He's the one who hurt me."

"I don't understand."

If ever a situation needed context, this one did. She'd teased Linc about holding the secret over his head, but Rose didn't see any other way out of this now. Maybe it was rationalizing, but shouldn't his sister know? The other woman got up and started to clear the table.

"You might want to sit down for this. It might come as a shock."

"What?" Ellie sat. "You're a man?"

"Wow, if that's where you went, I might need to change my brand of makeup." She was trying to lighten the mood but it wasn't happening. Quick was better. The way Linc had told her. "I'm just going to say this. Linc and I were married ten years ago."

"What?"

"We did meet at work. It was love at first sight—for me, at least. We went to Vegas and got married. It lasted fifteen minutes and he told me we were getting a divorce. That it was him, not me."

"Oh, God—" Ellie put a hand over her mouth and stared before adding, "He found out about his father."

"Yes, although he didn't tell me that then. Just that I was better off without him."

Ellie got up and filled a sippy cup with milk, then handed it to her daughter. The woman moved as if she was on automatic pilot and her mind was racing as she connected the dots. "You must have been—"

"Devastated. Hurt. After a while anger set in and got me through. Now?" She shrugged.

The other woman sat down across from her again. "You said he didn't tell you then. When *did* he tell you?"

"Just recently. He probably never would have except he found out that we're not divorced."

"What?" The pitch of her voice went up and got her daughter's attention. Leah started to cry so Ellie freed her from the chair and cuddled her close. "Mama's sorry, baby girl. But Uncle Linc is… I can't even think of a name bad enough to call him. How could you not be divorced?"

Rose explained everything and that he was handling it now. "In all fairness, he had a shock at the time he promised to take care of everything. Maybe you should cut him some slack."

"Slack?" Ellie snapped her fingers. "Slacker, maybe. There's a name and that's what he is. He's the one I'm going to hurt."

"Ellie, it's all right—"

"No, it's not. All this time you believed you were divorced, then he drops by out of the blue and says you're not? 'Oh, and by the way, will you decorate my condo?'"

"There was a little more in between." Although not all that much. "Basically that's what happened."

"Why didn't you slam the door in his face? I would have. I might now."

"Please don't. I really need this job." There was no point in trying to hide the truth so she explained that her business was in trouble. "Linc offered me this opportunity as a way to save it."

"A high-profile job." Ellie nodded as if pieces had just fallen into place. "So that's what he meant."

"About?" Rose prompted.

"Before he and Alex left today Linc said to tell you that he was going to talk to Burke and Sloan Holden about decorating the lobby of their new hotel."

"He did?"

"Yes. It was very specific, too. That you needed to know he was making good on his promise."

Oh, dear God. That made her feel awful and somehow it gave him an advantage. Because he was keeping his word and Rose had just spilled her guts.

Chapter Six

"Linc, please get here soon." Rose had prayed, willing him to walk in the door so she could talk to him before his sister did.

She'd tried his cell phone but only got voice mail. He'd told her service in the mountains was spotty and this was a superbad time to find out for herself that he was right. She'd taunted him about getting to watch the fallout when Ellie learned they were married but she never really planned to say anything.

It was just something to hold over his head for a little payback. In hindsight it had been pathetically easy for Ellie to get the information out of her, but the result was the same. The cat was out of the bag and there were going to be repercussions. All day it was like waiting for the other shoe to drop.

In spite of that hanging over her head, Rose had managed to get some work done on Linc's condo. Themes, sketches, ideas. But it hadn't been easy to concentrate. The office had a window to the front of the house with the long driveway and she kept looking out, waiting and watching.

She hoped to warn him that his sister knew their secret. Ellie had been gone all day; her job as an architect kept her pretty busy in this growing town. Rose only hoped she was a little busier today than Linc.

A few minutes later she heard a car and looked out the window to see his SUV pull in front of the house. He got out, all lean and lithe masculinity. She caught her breath, grateful that she was still sitting in the chair. Sometimes a wave of attraction to the man crashed over her and threatened to buckle her knees. This was one of those times.

"Pull it together," she muttered to herself.

The front door closed and she hurried to meet him in the two-story entryway. He set down his briefcase at the foot of the stairs and draped his navy blazer over the banister. In worn jeans and a long-sleeved powder-blue shirt that brought out the intensity of his blue eyes, he was sexier than sin. That was pretty darn inconvenient since sin was often irresistible. She felt another one of those attraction waves coming on and forced it away.

He smiled his oh-so gorgeous smile. "Wow. This is a nice thing."

"What?"

"You greeting me at the door after a long hard day at the office."

"Don't make this something it's not. And you don't have an office," she said.

"It's just nice to see you. Here at the front door. Just saying…" He walked past her and headed for the kitchen. "How was your day?"

"Fine." She shook off the dreamy thoughts that clouded her mind and caught up with him. "But—"

"Look at us, all domestic and diplomatic." He flipped on a wall switch and the kitchen's recessed lights instantly blazed to life. There was a satisfied gleam in his eyes and that was about to change.

"Linc, we need to talk—"

He put up a warning finger, cutting off her words. "Let me give you some advice. Those are words no man ever wants to hear within five minutes of walking in the door at night."

"Oh, for Pete's sake. Don't make this a thing—"

"I'm not. It's the truth. Ask Alex if you don't believe me. A guy doesn't want to hear it from anyone—man or woman. A conversation starting out like that is going to be a bad conversation. At least let me have a beer first."

"There may not be time for that. Quit being weird and just listen to me."

He reached into the refrigerator and grabbed a longneck. "Do you want one?"

"No." She needed a clear head for this.

He twisted off the cap and took a pull from the bottle, then met her gaze. "I'm in a great mood. You were wrong before. Alex and I now have an office and we looked at an amazing parcel of land. We're probably going to make an offer on it. That's a good thing and I'm just spreading happiness wherever I go."

"Oh, brother." Her voice was wry. "You're just a regular 'rainbows and unicorns' kind of guy. Any second you'll be tossing glitter."

"Make fun if you must. But how exactly is that being weird?"

"You're acting as if we're a couple. All like a husband coming home to the little woman. It's not natural and yet it sort of falls under the heading of what I need to talk to you about."

There was a puzzled look on his face as he studied her. "At the risk of sounding like a ten-year-old, it takes one to know one. You're the one acting weird. How was your day, really? I sincerely want to know. Think about it this way. I have a personal interest in what you're doing."

Even more than he realized, Rose thought. "I don't remember you being this wordy."

He shrugged. "I've evolved."

"Well, just stop it."

Beer bottle in hand he gestured toward her. "Now that's a momentous statement. How often does a man hear a woman telling him not to evolve? Next you'll be telling me *not* to get in touch with my feminine side.

In the background she heard the sound of the garage door going up and a car pulling in, and knew time was running out. "Will you just stop and listen to me. Ellie will be here any second—"

"I suppose so, since this is her house."

The inside door from the garage opened and closed. Moments later his sister came into the kitchen with Leah in her arms. She walked straight up to her brother and poked him in the chest with her index finger. "Lincoln Hart, you have a lot of explaining to do."

Boom. Time was up.

Rose sighed. "Now those are words a guy really doesn't want to hear."

He frowned at her, then met his sister's gaze. "What did I do?"

"You got married, that's what you did. Ten years ago, you took vows."

His mouth pulled tight for a moment, then his niece poked him in the chest, a perfect imitation of her mother. "See what you're teaching your child?"

Ellie set the little girl on her feet and she toddled off to the wicker basket in the family room, where her toys were stored. Her favorite game was to remove every last item from the very large basket and it would keep her busy for a while. That was a good thing, what with the tension arcing between her mother and uncle.

Rose felt horrible and wanted to do something to smooth out the rift. "This is all my fault."

"No," Ellie said. "My brother gets all the blame for this one."

Linc was clearly not happy when he glanced at Rose, and it was the first time she'd ever seen him look like that. Ten years ago there'd never been an angry moment between them. But, as he'd pointed out, he'd evolved. That didn't make her feel better.

He set his beer on the island beside him. "Ellie, calm down. You'll scare Leah."

"You're the one who should be scared. How could you fall in love and not tell me?"

"Really? That's where you're going with this? Because guys don't talk about every detail of their lives?"

Oh, boy, Rose thought. That was really a bad thing to say. Any minute she expected his sister's eyes to shoot fire and reduce him to ashes on the floor.

"That's wrong in so many ways that I don't even know where to start," Ellie said. "You got married. That's not just a detail, it's a life-changer. And I never knew."

"I don't know if it matters, but back then Linc and I agreed to keep us private for a little while," Rose interjected.

She wondered, not for the first time, if he'd suggested keeping it secret because he was ashamed of her and didn't want to tell his family since he didn't plan to stay married. And maybe she'd agreed to keep it hush-hush out of

fear that his family would object to him marrying a no-
body like her.

"You were so young and probably starry-eyed in love."
Ellie gave her a sympathetic look. "I know you're trying
to help, but this is all on Linc. He fell in love and took *the
step*. That's something you confide to someone you love
and have the sort of close relationship we do. Or maybe
I'm wrong about that."

"No, you're not. We are close," he protested.

Ellie planted her fists on her hips just as Leah ran over
and wrapped her chubby little arms around her mom's
jeans-clad leg. "I told you everything and you didn't share
anything. I'm very angry."

"Join the club." The fire in his eyes when he looked at
Rose was not unlike his sister's expression. "Rose called
me a jackass."

"Jackass," the little girl said, clear as a bell. "Jackass."

"Wow, thanks for that. You just taught my innocent little
girl to swear." Ellie huffed out a breath. "You get married
and separated, then disappear and teach my child to cuss?"

"In all fairness, Rose is the one who has every right to
be ticked off at me—"

"So do I." Ellie shook her head. "So do Mom and Dad
and the rest of your family. We love you. You grew up and
never suspected that you had a different father. Suddenly
this stranger shows up and we're dead to you?"

"You're exaggerating."

"I'm not. And you were gone for a long time. Without
ever saying a word about the fact that you got married."

"You were the one who talked me into coming back,"
he reminded her. "Only you could have."

"That's not going to work, Linc."

"Look, Ellie, you don't—"

"If you value your life, do not tell me that I don't understand. You're an ungrateful—"

"The word I think you're looking for is—" He looked down at the little girl who was staring at them with great interest. "J-a-c-k-a-s-s."

"Let's go with that. Leah doesn't need to expand her vocabulary with words that would shock moms and kids in her play group."

"I would never deliberately do anything to hurt you, Ellie. If you believe anything, believe that. I'm so very sorry."

The anger in Ellie's expression cracked. "Did Rose tell you to say that?"

"No." He glanced at her for a moment. "Why?"

"Because it was exactly the right thing to say and I didn't think you could come up with it on your own." She moved closer and put her arms around him, resting her cheek on his chest. "It's impossible to stay mad and keep yelling at you after that."

"Good." He kissed the top of her head, then looked at Rose, his expression unreadable. "I've evolved."

"Miracles do happen."

"Does that mean there's any chance that you're going to keep this to yourself?" he asked tentatively.

Ellie stepped away and started laughing. "Are you kidding? Have you met me?"

Just then Alex walked into the room. "Hi."

"Daddy!" Leah ran to him and he lifted her into his arms.

"Hi, little bit." He kissed and hugged his little girl, then looked at his wife. "How are my girls? Did you have a good day?"

"It was interesting," Ellie told him. "You're taking me

out to dinner so I can tell you all about it. Linc has volunteered to babysit."

"It's the least I can do," he agreed.

"For so many reasons." Ellie took the little girl from her husband and handed her to Linc. "If you say the magic words you just learned, maybe Rose will help. And, FYI, Leah has a dirty diaper."

Linc sniffed and the look on his face said Ellie wasn't lying about the diaper. And moments later her parents had left the building.

On the upside, Rose thought, the secret was out and the world hadn't come to an end. That didn't mean he wouldn't be furious with her for revealing it. The problem now was that she realized she cared whether or not he was angry with her.

Linc had no time to process the fact that Rose not only ratted him out to his sister, but also allowed him to be ambushed by said sibling. The part of his brain not dealing with the potential disaster of changing his niece's dirty diaper acknowledged that wasn't fair. She'd been trying to tell him something but he was—how did she put it?—wordy.

He looked down at Leah, who, thank God, was on the changing table and quietly preoccupied with the car keys he'd given her. "Princess, do you think I'm wordy?"

She nodded, then held out her little hand and said, "Key."

"Right you are. Uncle Linc is going to change your diaper."

"I make poop." She grinned proudly.

"Yes, you did."

He undid the fasteners on her denim overalls and slid them off. Like any good military general planning a mission he assessed supplies. Wipes and spare diapers were stacked beneath the table, at his fingertips. That didn't make him feel any less like a water buffalo at high tea in this pink room with its pictures of fairies and princesses. The furniture was white and the hand pulls were decorated with pink rosebuds. Leah still slept in a crib, but there was a canopy bed just waiting for her to be old enough to sleep in it.

But looking around was just putting off the inevitable. He took a deep breath and held it, then undid the diaper and cleaned off the little bottom. Next to the changing table was a magic container that inhibited odors. He dropped it in there.

"Good news, kid. The worst is done."

"Good job." The little girl clapped her hands.

"Thank you. Obviously you are showered with positive reinforcement."

She was a mirror of her mother. Case in point, poking him in the chest. He knew words of praise were something she heard frequently.

"Linc?"

He glanced over his shoulder. Rose was standing in the doorway. "What?"

"Ellie called and said to give Leah a bath since you're—" She indicated the clean-up operation currently in progress. "You know."

"Yeah."

"She told me where the pajamas are and to make macaroni and cheese and green beans for Leah's dinner. If you're okay with it, I'll handle that."

"Okay. What about food for the adults?"

"For you there's leftover pot roast to reheat. Mine is easy. Bread and water." She moved to the white dresser and pulled out pink pajamas and white socks, then set them on the bed. "I'll go fill the tub for her, then get dinner ready."

Without another word she left and moments later he heard the sound of running water from the next room.

"Okay, kid, I'm flying solo on this and would greatly appreciate your full cooperation in this endeavor. Okay?"

"Okay," she answered enthusiastically.

After hearing the water go off, Linc took her into the bathroom and lifted her into the tub. Sitting on the side was a plastic cup, which she grabbed before plopping herself down. After filling it with water she dumped it over her head.

"'Poo," she said pointing to a bottle beside her.

At first he thought she had to go again but eventually realized she meant the container that proclaimed in no uncertain terms that the shampoo would not sting her eyes. He handed it over and kneeled down beside her.

"Go for it, kid." She responded with a string of words that he was pretty sure meant thank you and said his name. He loved the way it sounded coming from her. "I'll wash your hair."

"No." She shook her head and water went flying. "Me. I big girl."

"Excellent," he said. "An independent woman."

Linc let her handle things, partly because he never said no to her and partly because this bath thing didn't have to be perfect. There was soap, water and he was there to make sure she was safe. He called that a win.

A pink towel was set out by the tub, probably by Rose. Another independent woman. He was still pissed off that she'd sold him out, but had to admit she didn't jump ship on the babysitting. She pitched in and didn't have to. This wasn't in her job description.

He let the water out of the tub and that set off his niece.

"No, Unc 'Inc. Me do."

"Sorry, kid." He put the plug down again, before all

the water was gone and let her do it her way. Not unlike the woman who was now making dinner. He wrapped the child in a towel and lifted her out, noting the tangle of her wet hair. "Can you comb your hair?"

"No. Brush."

"Gotcha." He held her up to mirror height and let her do the job. It wasn't perfect, but no way he was telling her that. "You look beautiful."

In her room he put her back on the changing table. After a couple of tries he managed to get a diaper on her and she insisted on putting herself in the pajamas.

"Are you hungry?"

She nodded. "Go see Wo'?"

"Rose?" When she nodded vigorously he held out his hand and she put her little one into it. "Let's go."

Rose was at the stove filling a three-section plastic plate. She looked at them and a soft expression chased away the frown on her face. "Leah, you look all clean."

"She did it all by herself," Linc said.

"Good job."

Hmm. Was that a chick thing or a mom thing? A puzzle for another time, he thought. "Okay, princess, let's get you in the chair."

It was a joint effort—he set her on it and Rose clicked the plastic tray into place. Then she put the plate and small fork on it and the little girl dug in. The two of them looked at each other and breathed a sigh of relief.

"Thanks for the help," he said. "I didn't expect it."

"I'm not the one who walks away, Linc. That's your default behavior."

This payback was starting to get old. Especially after what she did. "Is that why you told Ellie? To get even with me?"

"Of course not. I—"

"You promised not to say anything, Rose."

"No, I didn't. I only said it was pretty awesome having something to hold over your head."

"And how much you'd enjoy watching when Ellie found out. Well, chalk one off your to-do list. Was it as entertaining as you expected?"

"Actually, no." Her look was defiant. "I didn't like seeing Ellie upset."

"Me, either." He met her gaze. "So why did you spill the beans?"

"She started to ask questions. How long ago we met. She mentioned you never said anything about me and yet you remembered all the details of how I like my coffee. Then she connected that we met right around the time your biological father contacted you." She sighed. "Did you really think we could be here together and your sister wouldn't notice that there was *something* between us?"

"Yes." That was a knee-jerk response because stubborn was his middle name.

Rose shook her head as if to say he was dumb as dirt. "She's smart. She knows you better, I think, than you know yourself and she's a woman. We don't miss much."

"So now she knows and my relationship with her will never be what it was."

"Oh, for Pete's sake. Why is everything with you an absolute?" she demanded. "There can't be a disagreement with your sister and then you both put it away and move on like you were before?"

"No." Again Mr. Stubborn. "This was a major breach of confidence and she'll never get over it."

"Yeah," Rose said drily. "I could tell by the way she hugged you, then left her child in your care."

When she put it like that… "She was just really ticked

off and not thinking straight. When she has a chance to mull it over she's really going to be mad."

"Baloney." Rose shook her head. "If this revelation had pushed her over the edge, she would have kicked you out of her house."

"She didn't because you're here," he argued.

"No, she would have done it and let me stay." Her smile was full of confidence as she folded her arms over her chest. "She likes me. Possibly more than you, at least right now."

"You're probably right about that," he admitted. "Throwing me into the deep end of the pool with a toxic diaper and a bath was the ultimate punishment."

Rose studied the front of him, soaked with bathwater. "I think you're a fraud."

"You've made that pretty clear, but what is it this time?"

"You enjoyed spending time with that little girl. There was laughter and it didn't sound a whole lot like punishment to me. I heard the two of you chattering away."

"She started it."

"Right." Rose smiled, then it faded, replaced by a sad expression. "You'd be a great father, Linc."

"No."

"You refuse to see it, but Ellie's right. The father who raised you did it so well you never suspected you weren't his son. That means he treated all four of his children the same way."

"My sister wants to pretend nothing is different. But it is. I can never un-know the truth."

"It doesn't have to define you. It doesn't have to close you off to loving someone." Her mouth pulled tight for a moment. "But loving is hard. Running is much easier."

"It's not fair to judge." He knew it had been foolish to ask her to forgive and forget. That was never going to happen and it made him angry. "People deal with adversity differently."

"Stuff happens. How you deal with it reveals character," she insisted.

"That's just it. Half of my DNA is a blank. I don't know who I am."

"Then find out." She smiled at Leah, who was using her little princess fork to carefully move macaroni from the plate to her mouth. If there was a mishap she just picked it up off the tray and shoved the food in. Rose met his gaze again and hers held a hint of warning. "If you don't make an effort and do something proactive, you're going to hold back and miss out on the best that life has to offer."

"Now that I'm not being lied to and have all the facts, it's my choice whether or not I pursue this."

"You're right. No one else has a say in what you do." She looked at him for several moments, then sighed. "We can only take responsibility for our own actions. So, in that spirit… I'm sorry I told Ellie. The other alternative was to flat-out lie and I couldn't do that. But I didn't do it to get even with you. That much energy would mean that I still care about you. Just so we're clear, I don't care about you anymore."

She brushed by him then and walked over to the refrigerator, pulling out leftover containers to reheat last night's dinner.

Linc was annoyed again and the reason was even more annoying. He cared that she didn't care about him. Damn it, he really did.

What the hell was that?

Chapter Seven

The next morning Rose was waiting for Linc in his sister's home office. At breakfast she'd explained that input from him was now required to do her job. After what happened last night she wasn't entirely sure he still wanted her on the job, and if not she needed to know that, too.

He walked in at the appointed time. "Let's do this."

"First, we should talk about whether or not you can work with me. I know you're mad about what I said to Ellie—"

"Not anymore." His expression was unreadable and that was irritating.

"I'm not sure I believe you."

"Why is that?" He folded his arms over his chest and met her gaze.

"If you haven't been taken over by aliens and you're the same Lincoln Hart who has held a grudge against his parents for the last ten years, it seems out of character that you would get over the fact that I revealed our secret marriage from a decade ago just yesterday."

One corner of his mouth quirked up. "Ellie seems to be over it and so am I."

"So you still want me to do the interior design on your condo?"

"Yes."

"Good." That was such a relief. She held out a hand and indicated the two club chairs in front of the desk in the home office. Her laptop was there. "Have a seat. I want to show you some living room ideas and get your feedback."

"Why can't you throw some stuff together and I'll pick something out?"

"Do you have somewhere more important to be?" She tilted her head.

"I'm busy and—"

"If you don't want flowers, puppies and flocked wallpaper in your personal space, you're going to want to sit down and work with me on this. It's my goal to see that when the job is complete, you're deliriously happy with your space."

"Fine." He sat, clearly impatient.

That should have bugged her and it did a little, but mostly the behavior reminded her of a little boy who didn't get his way. For an instant, she could picture what a child of theirs might have been like. That made her sad, so she went back to being bugged.

"Okay. The sooner we get started, the sooner you can go be a tycoon." She sat beside him. "I'm going to click through these design ideas and try to pin down what you like. Color schemes. Ambience, setting, that sort of thing."

"I just want it done," he grumbled.

"You can't possibly want that more than I do." It was

hard to be with him and bump painfully into the past every day, to have her face rubbed in what might have been.

Linc lifted an eyebrow questioningly. "Are you anxious to get back to your regularly scheduled life?"

"Yes and no."

"Hmm." For some reason those words made his bored look disappear. "I'd like to hear about the *no* part. What makes you not eager to get back?"

"It's beautiful here. I like the town and people I've met so far. And there's the prospect of more work."

"Yes. Don't think it escaped my notice that I kept my end of the bargain and spoke to Burke and Sloan Holden about your job skills while you were stabbing me in the back."

"I explained that," she protested.

"Yes, you did." He relaxed back into the club chair. "So it's work and nothing to do with me that would keep you here."

She wouldn't let it be about him. "Wow, how did I never notice that your ego is the size of a long-haul truck?"

"I've never tried to hide who I am."

True, she thought. His problem was that half his family story was missing and even a guy as confident as Linc would find that disconcerting.

"Then I guess the reason I didn't notice was my problem. I was starry-eyed and that tends to prevent a girl from seeing clearly."

"You are refreshing. A woman who takes responsibility." He grinned suddenly, and it was spectacular. "So if you like Blackwater Lake and are looking forward to more work here, what would make your life in Texas beckon?" The words were barely out of his mouth when he snapped his fingers. "Chandler. I almost forgot about him. He's why you're in a hurry to get back."

"Yes." The answer was automatic and also a lie. She hadn't really thought about him much and rationalized that Linc was bigger than life and dealing with him was a whirlwind that sucked all the oxygen out of the room. There was no time or energy for anything else. "And we need to work."

"Right." There wasn't a lot of enthusiasm in the single word, not like he'd shown when he brought up her personal life.

She directed his attention to the laptop monitor. "I'm going to scroll through these living-room design ideas and I want you to tell me what, if anything, you like." She clicked and brought up an image.

"Too cold."

"Okay." The ceilings and walls were white and there was an area rug under a glass-topped table. "You're decisive. That's good. Next."

He carefully studied a couple of pictures, then pointed to one. "I like the wood-beam ceiling and built-in bookcases."

"Me, too," she said. "But I'm not sure about that in your living room. Let's keep it in mind for your home office."

His expression said great idea. "Sounds good."

She clicked on the next shot. "Now in this one I like the crown molding and the color of the walls. Gray and white are being used a lot right now but I'm not sure about it for you."

"Why?"

"I've been researching pictures of Blackwater Lake, all the seasons. In winter there's a lot of snow and fog in the mountains. I think the interior of your home should be a contrast to a time of the year that some people might find depressing. Earth colors might give you a warmer ambience overall. And there can be variations on the shade in other rooms that make it less gloomy."

"Good point."

She tapped her lip looking at the next picture. "The TV in this one is prominent in the great room. Since you're going to have a media room do you want one in the family room, too?"

He thought for a moment. "Maybe."

"Would it be a distraction there when you're entertaining?"

"I don't do much of that."

"Not even the family? For football games or holidays?"

"No." He met her gaze. "It's saying a lot that I would rather talk paint color and built-in bookshelves than personal issues, so make whatever you want out of it and we can just move on."

"Okay, then. Next picture." It had white fuzzy chairs against a navy blue wall and both of them said together, "No way."

Rose laughed. "That was unprofessional of me. You might have loved and desperately wanted that. I'm not supposed to influence your choices."

"Not even to talk me out of a big mistake?"

"I would point out the pros and cons without making my preference known," she said.

There was a look in his eyes that was both intense and impossible to read. "No, please, reveal preferences. I'm paying you the big bucks so you'll keep me from picking out something hideous. I want you to like it."

"It doesn't matter whether I do or not. I'm not going to live there."

"Right."

Had she just seen something in his face? A vulnerability, or longing? She wasn't sure and didn't want to make a big deal out of it. After clicking on the next picture she asked, "What do you think?"

"Looks cheesy."

"I agree." But she pointed to the wood floor. "That's a nice color. Not too dark or light and it's pine. Seems appropriate for the mountains. What do you think?"

He examined it closer. "Yeah. I'd have missed it because the rest of the room turned me off. You really have an eye for detail."

"It's my job. And occasionally I'm right." The next five shots were unhelpful but the sixth one caught his eye. She could tell by the excitement in his expression. "What?"

"That fireplace. It's classic but simple and warm."

"Look at you throwing around decorating lingo." She studied the white wood and detailed edges of the fireplace. "I'd have figured you for a rock-face kind of guy. And we should look at that, too. Because this is a focal point of the room and the rest of your choices need to complement it if that's most important to you."

"Important to me," he repeated, studying her. His eyes turned intense and their faces were very close together.

Rose felt heat creep into her cheeks and her pulse rate kicked up a notch or two. She would give almost anything to know what he was thinking and thought about asking straight out. But her cell phone on the desk rang. Normally she checked the identity of the caller before answering but she was too grateful for the interruption.

She picked up the device and hit Talk. "Rose Tucker."

"Hey, Rosie."

"Chandler." She met Linc's gaze and saw the "I told you so" wheels turning. Distance. She needed to be away from him. After standing, she moved toward the doorway. "How are you?"

"Missing you."

"That's sweet." This was where she should have said she missed him, too. But she didn't.

"How's it going there?" If Chandler noticed her lack of reciprocation, his voice didn't reveal anything.

She had told him about the out-of-town job and since he knew nothing about her and Linc being married, the question had to be about her work. "Good. Things are fine."

"How much longer will you be gone?"

"Hard to say." She glanced over her shoulder and saw Linc not even trying to pretend that he wasn't listening to every word. "This is a big job."

"Can you get away for a weekend here in Dallas?"

"Not likely."

"What if I put together a couple of days and come to you?"

Oh, that was a very bad idea and she just barely stopped the words from coming out of her mouth. Instead she thought carefully about what to say. "I hate to see you do that. I won't be able to spend much time with you." In a sudden and surprising flash of insight she saw that Linc looked awfully pleased about that. Was she pleased about his reaction? After telling him she didn't care? That would make her a liar.

"Chandler, I'd love to chat longer, but I'm with a client. Can I call you later?"

"Sure. I look forward to it. Love you, Rose."

"Thanks for calling." She ended the call and took a deep breath before turning to Linc. "Okay, where were we?"

"We're where I ask how important that guy really is to you."

"Very." She sat down and met his gaze, stubbornly refusing to look away even though she desperately wanted to do just that. And she had a feeling he could see the blush creeping into her cheeks.

"Very important?" He leaned closer. "I don't think I believe you. That sounded an awful lot like a defensive response ten years in the making."

"Oh, please." She made a dismissive noise. "Chandler and I are practically engaged. I told you that."

"Then why did you discourage him from coming for a visit?" He held up a hand to stop her protest. "It was the part where you said you couldn't spend much time with him that clued me in. So why don't you want to see him?"

"That's none of your business, Linc."

"Funny." He glanced down for a moment, a small smile on his lips. "It sure feels like my business."

"Well, it's not. Now let's get back to work." She reached out and clicked the computer mouse to scroll to the next picture. "What do you think of this one?"

"What would you do if I kissed you?"

Her heart stopped for a second, then resumed beating very hard and fast. She couldn't look at him. "Don't you dare. I have a boyfriend."

"But what if I did? Would you slap my face?"

"You're so unimportant to me it wouldn't be worth getting that worked up over."

"Care to bet?"

Pulling herself together, she finally met his gaze. She didn't care about him, so why not? "You're on."

He reached into his jeans pocket, pulled out a twenty-dollar bill and set it on the desk. Then he stood and reached down to take her hands and lift her to her feet. He cupped her face in his palms and brushed his thumbs over her cheekbones until she thought she couldn't breathe. And when he touched his mouth to hers, she swore fireworks were going off nearby.

He moved his lips over her face with small, nibbling kisses and touched the tip of his tongue to her bottom lip, tracing it slowly, erotically. Dear God, it felt so good. Right now she'd give him another twenty dollars not to stop doing what he was doing. But that wasn't to be. He pulled back and she swore the move was reluctant on his part. At least she wasn't the only one breathing hard.

Linc looked at her, dropped his hands and stepped away. "Okay, go ahead and slap me. After all, you have a boyfriend."

Oh, God! Chandler. One second she'd held him up as a shield, the next he'd been wiped from her mind like an annoying computer virus. This was a problem and she needed to take care of it right away.

In the Prosper, Texas, diner near her design studio and apartment Rose looked at the man sitting across the table. "Thanks for coming, Chandler."

"Are you kidding? No way I'd have missed this." He smiled warmly and settled his hand on hers. "Although I have to admit it was a surprise when you called and asked me to meet you. After our phone conversation the other day I had no idea when I would see you again."

That talk was before Linc kissed her. The kiss had changed everything. It hadn't taken her long to know what she had to do. After letting Linc know she'd be gone for a couple days she caught a flight to Dallas and here she was with Chandler. One look at him confirmed that the simple touch of Linc's lips to hers was more powerful than anything she'd ever felt with this man.

"Well—" she shrugged "—here I am."

"Yes." He turned his hand over and snuggled her fingers into his palm. "Here you are."

The man was handsome, charming, smart, funny and kind. He was terrific and as far as she could tell had only one flaw. He wasn't Lincoln Hart.

She slid her hand from his. "Chandler, we need to talk—"

"I think you felt it, too," he interrupted.

"I'm sorry, what?"

"You know. They say absence makes the heart grow fonder. Since you've been gone, I realized how much I really care about you. I—"

"Hey, you two." Janie Tucker stood at the end of the table. She was working her shift at the diner and seemed pleased. The smile made her look younger and put a twinkle in her blue eyes. Dark hair the same shade as Rose's was cut into a short bob. "Good to see you, Chandler."

"You, too, Janie."

"Can I get you something to drink?"

"I think we need a couple of minutes. Do you mind?" Chandler gave her the smile that broke every female heart except Rose's.

"Sure thing." She walked back to the counter.

Her mom didn't know what was going on and Rose wanted to keep it that way until she broke the news to this man. When they were alone she sighed and met his gaze. "The thing is this job has turned out to be more complicated than I expected."

"I guess that means I'm going to miss you longer than we expected."

If it was just about time and distance, he'd be right. But it was all about that kiss. "There's something else."

"Whatever it is, I'll be there to work it out with you. That's what a significant other does. And I think you know I want to be more than that. I want to marry you."

"Oh, Chandler—"

He smiled, mistaking her distress for something else that encouraged him. "I've been looking at engagement rings and I want to ask—"

"Don't." She held up a hand to stop him.

"What?"

"Don't ask me. Don't say the words. Please, Chandler," she begged.

"I can't help it. I have to. Will you marry me, Rose?"

She shook her head. "I can't."

"Of course you can. The job in Montana won't last forever. We'll figure out a way to make it work. All you have to do is say yes."

"I can't."

"You keep saying that." His excitement slipped, giving way to confusion. "Why?"

She blew out a long breath and it flashed through her mind that Linc must have experienced a little dread like this before he told her about not being divorced. But he was the last person she wanted to think about right now. If he'd just kept his mouth to himself...

"Rose?"

"I'm married."

"You're what?" Chandler blinked at her. "I don't understand. You're joking."

"I wish," she said miserably.

"Married? If you don't want to marry me just say so. There's no need to lie to me—"

"It's the truth."

"I don't understand. Why didn't you tell me before?"

"I didn't know. I thought I was divorced." She explained what happened ten years ago—falling in love, the quick marriage, what felt like a quicker split with very little explanation from her husband. Why there was no divorce, although it was progressing now. "Linc promised he would take care of it this time and get it right."

"And you believe him?"

"Yes." Trust him, no. "He wants this over with as much as I do."

"Lincoln Hart is your husband?" Chandler frowned. "Is he the man you're working for now? In Montana?"

"Yes."

"What's going on, Rose?" It was not a voice he'd ever used with her. "Is there still something between you?"

"No!" At least she hoped not.

"But you agreed to go with him to Montana. And didn't think it was necessary to tell me you're married to him."

"You know my business is in trouble," she said.

"And I offered to help."

"It's something I have to do alone." Every instinct she had told her not to let him, which, in hindsight, was a sign of something not right. "Vicki said I should tell you about the divorce. It was my decision alone to—"

"So your friend knew the truth but you didn't think it was important to tell me?"

"I should have. I know. I just didn't think that—"

"What? I'd ever find out?" He dragged his fingers through perfectly cut dark blond hair. "So he married you under false pretenses to get you into bed and now you lied to me."

"I didn't overtly tell you an untruth." It was a small hair but she split it anyway.

"A lie of omission." His lips pulled tight for a moment. "The two of you should be very happy together. You're cut from the same cloth."

Rose knew he was right, although not about her and Linc being happy together. "Chandler, please listen. Let me try to explain."

"Try? How much more can there be? No. I'm done." He glared at her. "But I have one question and you owe me the courtesy of the truth."

"Anything."

"Why not just tell me this when we talked the other day?"

Because Linc was sitting there listening to every word. "At that moment I didn't plan to break up. There was a lot to think about—"

"Or," he interrupted. "Better yet you could have called it quits in a text."

Rose winced. She probably had that coming. He had every right to be bitter and though she wanted to get up and walk out right this minute, she didn't. Chandler wouldn't want to hear it, but the real reason she was here had to do with Linc. He'd had the decency to tell her to her face that they were over and she couldn't do less.

And she wouldn't make this worse for Chandler by revealing that after kissing Linc she realized if she had forever-after feelings for Chandler another man's touch wouldn't have affected her the way it did. There had been signs that it wasn't right but her mom really liked him and Rose wasn't getting any younger. Wishful thinking collided with reality the moment Linc's mouth touched hers.

"I'm so sorry." She met his angry gaze. "I didn't mean to hurt you."

"Go to hell, Rose."

It was a technicality, but she didn't need to "go" anywhere because she was already in hell. "Chandler—"

He slid out of the booth and didn't look back as he passed her obviously puzzled mother and headed straight to the diner's exit.

Moments later Janie was heading her way. Too late Rose realized she hadn't carefully thought through the location for this meeting.

"What's going on, Rose? Why did Chandler leave so suddenly? He looked really upset." Janie glanced toward the door he'd stormed through just a minute ago. "What did you say to him?"

"I broke things off."

"But why?"

"I'm not in love with him."

"Are you sure? Maybe if you gave it a little longer." Janie sat down in the booth.

"I'm sure, Mom. When you know, you know." With Linc it had been like an electric storm, immediate and powerful. That made it all the more painful when he left her.

"Does this have anything to do with that man you're working for?"

There was a lot of potential here for yet another lie. Ten years ago Linc was the only one who knew she'd married him. Even her mother was in the dark. Rose always intended to tell her but then it was over and she'd believed the heavy burden of foolishness was hers to carry alone.

"Mom, there's something you need to know."

As Rose talked, a series of emotions drifted over Janie's still-pretty face. Shock, anger, sympathy and, worst of all, a mother's helplessness to fix her child's trouble.

There was so much disappointment in Janie's voice when she said, "You could have told me, honey."

"Yeah. I should have. I'm sorry." Apparently it was the night for those two words.

"You didn't have to go through all of that alone. I should have been there for you."

"You always are, Mom." She reached over and took the other woman's worn hand. "It's just— You work so hard. I didn't want to put one more worry on you."

"You're sweet." She squeezed her daughter's fingers. "But I'm tough. And so are you. Always remember if you need me I'm there and together we can handle anything."

"Okay."

"I mean it." She almost smiled. "Don't get me wrong. I'm still pretty mad at you. But that doesn't change the fact that I love you more than anything in this world."

"I love you, too, Mom." It occurred to her that Linc's sister said almost the same thing to him.

"Now tell me about this guy you're working for. The one you're still married to."

"There's not much to say—"

"No. Not getting away with that again." Janie shook her head. "When you left Texas things with you and Chandler were practically perfect. After a short time in Montana you come back here to break up with him? I know there's a few years on me but I'm not that out of touch. Something happened and now is as good a time as any to break the pattern of keeping things to yourself."

So Rose told her mother about kissing Linc and found sharing the burden helped in an unexpected way. It became clear why she hadn't called it quits with Chandler on the phone. She didn't want Linc to know about the breakup. The idea of her being involved with someone might be the only thing that stood between her and falling for Linc again.

That was called making the same mistake twice and only a card-carrying fool would do that. He didn't have to know that she no longer had a boyfriend.

Chapter Eight

Rose had left Blackwater Lake after giving Linc some vague excuse and now he was wandering aimlessly around his sister's kitchen while said sister was preparing dinner. More often than not he was in Ellie's way, but at the moment she stood in front of a wooden cutting board and pounded the living daylights out of a perfectly innocent boneless skinless chicken breast.

It occurred to him that hitting something might be just what he needed. "Hey, El, want me to do that for you?"

She met his gaze. "That offer sounds an awful lot like a cry for help."

"What are you talking about?"

"You look like testosterone central, which is code for wanting to put your fist through a wall."

"I do not."

"Do to. You've had that look on your face ever since Rose left." She smacked the chicken, then looked up. "Where is she anyway?"

"Home. Something about taking care of an issue and seeing her mother." Every time he thought about her evasive answer his gut knotted with irritation.

"Linc?"

"Hmm?" He blinked and focused on his sister.

"I was talking to you."

"Sorry." He didn't bother to share the train of thought that distracted him. "What did you say?"

"Is Rose coming back? Or did she come to her senses and figure out what a toad you are?"

"Funny." His niece came toddling over and held her arms out to be picked up. He was happy to oblige. "Your mom is a funny girl, princess. She called me a name."

A fitting one since he was the frog who'd kissed Rose. Frog? Toad? Same difference. But didn't they say you had to kiss a lot of frogs before finding your prince? Again he thought it best not to share the information.

"So is she?" Ellie persisted. "Coming back, I mean."

"She didn't say she wasn't. And I have a signed contract for her to decorate my condo. I'm going to hold her to it." He looked at Leah. "Right?"

"Wight." She nodded vigorously.

"It's unanimous. If she doesn't provide mutually agreed upon services, I can sue her."

"That's productive. Go straight to the bad place." Ellie gave him her patented "you're an idiot" stare. "Have you called her?"

"Once or twice." He'd struck up quite a friendship with her voice-mail message and now her mailbox was full.

"And?"

"She didn't pick up."

"What did you do, Linc?"

"Why would you go there? Does it have to be my fault?" He looked at Leah. "Does it?"

"Yes," she said.

"See." Ellie looked triumphant. "Even an almost-three-year-old gets it."

"Traitor," he said to Leah, who just grinned at him.

This argument was on shaky footing because he was almost sure that kiss was the catalyst for her disappearance. And it had nothing to do with toads and frogs. He'd challenged her and they kissed. It didn't take a relationship genius to know there was something going on between her and the boyfriend and it wasn't love.

And, yes, he was aware he'd taken advantage of the situation but it was in the spirit of doing her a favor. If the guy was right for her she wouldn't have been affected. And she had been. On the flip side of that coin, he'd been affected, too. It was official. He really, *really* wanted her.

Ellie sighed. "Why is it so hard for you to just admit you still have feelings for Rose?"

"It's not hard. I freely admit to having feelings. Let me count the ways. Annoyance, irritation, vexation, exasperation, frustration—"

"You're just being a stubborn—" She stopped and looked at her daughter. "J-a-c-k-a-s-s."

"Takes one to know one."

"You like her, Linc."

He was feeling backed into a corner. "What is this? Junior high?"

"Clearly not. Those kids have more maturity than you do."

"Wow. Hostile environment," he said.

"The atmosphere here in my home is just fine. You're the hostile one." She smiled at her daughter. "Leah, Uncle Linc could sure use a hug. He's sad."

He wanted to tell his sister what she could do with

her hostile environment, but two chubby little arms came around his neck.

"Don't cwy, Unca 'Inc."

"Okay." He hugged her back as a lump suddenly formed in his throat. He wanted one of these little people but... There was always a damn *but*. He kissed the little girl's cheek. "Thanks, princess."

"Welcome."

He set her down. "I'm going out."

"Me go, too?" Leah looked up hopefully.

"Next time," he promised. "Bar None doesn't allow anyone under twenty-one."

"That's a great idea." Ellie smiled approvingly. "It's ladies' night. Happy hour prices are good for single women all night. You're unattached. Do the math."

"Have I ever told you how aggravating you are?"

"Every day. But you love me anyway."

"I do." He kissed her forehead, then headed for the front door, where his car keys were in the basket on a side table next to it. He called out, "Don't wait up."

Laughter drifted to him. "In your dreams."

A short time later Linc pulled into the parking lot at the local drinking establishment. The sign over the roof had crossed cocktail glasses, while neon lights in a window spelled out Beer. There was no mistaking the purpose of this place.

He got out of the SUV and chirped it locked, then walked up to the heavy double doors and grabbed one of the vertical handles to open it. The bar and grill was crowded. There were a lot of ladies sitting at the bistro tables scattered around the center of the room and couples occupying booths lining the perimeter. He stood just inside the door for several moments, scoping out everything, and didn't see an empty chair or stool at the bar against the wall.

So, to sum up, he was oh for two. He couldn't take out his frustration on the chicken and now every seat in the bar was occupied. He'd apparently ticked off fate and she was getting even with him.

He was about to turn around and leave when a redhead approached him.

"Hi."

"Hi. Is it always this crowded in here?"

"I wish. It's my place. Delanie Carlson." She held out her hand and he shook it. "But I get a good crowd on ladies' night."

"I can see that. Standing room only. I'm Linc Hart."

"Nice to meet you. My friends and I were wondering if you'd like to join us. We can squeeze in another person. Unless you're determined to be by yourself and brood?" She angled her head at a table in the corner, where two attractive women were sitting.

"The brooding can wait," he said. "Lead the way."

She did and stopped at the table where the two women waited. She held out her hand and indicated the one with short, blond hair and blue eyes. "This is Lucy Bishop. She's the cook and co-owner of the Harvest Café."

"Lincoln Hart."

Delanie looked at the other woman, who had auburn hair and really stunning turquoise eyes. She was wearing a navy skirt and matching suit jacket with a white blouse. Very professional. Probably came directly from work.

"Linc, this is Hadley Michaels, manager and events coordinator at the Blackwater Lake Lodge."

"Nice to meet you," she said.

"Same here." He smiled at each of them. "Do you mind if I join you?"

"Absolutely not."

"Please do."

"What'll you have?" Delanie asked.

"Beer. Tap."

"Coming right up." She shrugged. "I have connections. Take my chair. I'll get another one from the back."

She walked away and Linc looked at the two very attractive ladies and thought, Rose who? Coming here was a good idea, not that he would confirm that to his sister. "I appreciate you letting me crash the party."

"It looked like you were going to leave," Lucy said. "If we let a handsome man like you get away, that doesn't say much for our skills. And make no mistake. We do have skills."

Hadley shook her head. "She makes the best quiche I've ever tasted, but her flirting muscles are a little rusty."

"Really? Was it that obvious?" Lucy teased.

"Not to me." He liked straightforward. No games. No lines drawn in the sand. No history. Don't go there, he warned. It was single ladies' night at Bar None.

"Here you go." Delanie put a cocktail napkin on the table, then set his glass of beer on it. One of the employees brought a chair and she settled herself into it and held up her glass. "To a new friend."

"Who's a man," Lucy added.

"And outnumbered in the best possible way." He touched his glass to theirs.

"Now who's flirting?" Lucy gave her auburn-haired friend a raised eyebrow.

"Don't pay any attention to her," Delanie said. "We'll be gentle."

"So this is your night off?" he asked.

"I'm a single lady." She lifted one shoulder. "For this I have part-time help so I can hang out with my friends."

"And pick up men. Ones who look a little lost." Hadley toyed with the stem of her wineglass. "Is there any particular reason you look that way?"

"Does it have anything to do with that interior decorator from Dallas?" Lucy grinned. "I have a restaurant. People come in and talk. And I know your sister, Ellie."

"So much for being gentle with him." Hadley looked sympathetic. "Don't mind them. They can't help themselves. It's what happens when politeness and curiosity bump together."

"It's a small town," he said. "And the best part is that I don't even have to talk. You're handling that for me like the pros you are."

"Nice try." Lucy sipped her pink drink. "Were you looking lost over a lady or not?"

"Or not," he said.

"Okay, then." Hadley nodded and changed the subject to town expansion and his role in it.

Linc ended up ordering food and chatting with the three of them the entire evening. They were all beautiful, smart funny women and he wasn't interested in hitting on any of them. Because not one was Rose.

Apparently this was what poetic justice felt like. Ten years ago he'd done the leaving and felt bad enough. Tonight he found out being the one who got left really sucked.

Rose left Dallas on an oh-dark-thirty flight to Helena, then had to wait half the day for her connection to Blackwater Lake. It was a very different experience from her first trip here on the private jet. She'd texted Linc that she was coming back today, but not the time. So it was a surprise to see him waiting for her in baggage claim.

At DFW Airport she could have easily slipped by him in a crowd, but this newly opened terminal was proportional to the small town. There was no way he would miss her. Besides employees and the few passengers on the puddle jumper with her, she and Linc were the only two people there at just past seven in the evening.

She had no choice but to stop in front of him and get this first meeting over with. If only she could keep her heart from beating so fast. "Hi, Linc."

"Welcome back."

"Thanks. Why are you here?"

"To pick you up."

When she had talked to Ellie and explained about needing a couple of personal days, his sister had teased that a break was understandable. Working with Linc was intense and anyone who did automatically qualified for sainthood. The guest room would be waiting for her when she got back.

Rose hadn't given him the flight information on purpose, hoping to have other people around when she saw him again. "How did you know when I'd be coming in?"

"You told me it would be today. Since all flights come to Blackwater Lake through Helena and there's only one, I connected the dots."

"You didn't have to meet me."

He took the handle of her rolling bag and started walking. "It's the least I could do."

His tone seemed conciliatory, as if he knew working with him was a challenge. And it was. That kiss had been a dare. It was about messing with her and the relationship she had. *Had* being the operative word. The tactic worked because there was no more her and Chandler.

He had every right to be hurt and she'd hated doing that to him, especially since she knew how it felt. But letting things go on when she didn't love him would have compounded his pain and resentment. Thanks to Linc, she knew that, too.

"Rose?" He opened the glass door leading to the parking lot. "Why did you go to Texas?"

Oh, boy.

She met his gaze and said, "I'm not going to answer that."

He stared at her as she walked past him, head held high. "Seriously? I expected you to at least say something like… 'it's complicated.'"

"I wish I'd thought of it." The air was crisp and cool, missing the humidity of Texas. There was a faint pine smell, even here at the airport. In spite of the tension with Linc, her spirits lifted as they crossed the nearly deserted street to the parking lot.

"What do you have to hide?" He glanced down.

The thought crossed her mind to tell him she'd visited her mother, which was true. But she knew Linc and there would have been a cross examination, including a question about whether or not she'd seen Chandler. Somehow he would get the truth out of her and she couldn't have that.

"This is really none of your business."

"It kind of is." He hit a button on his key fob and the rear hatch of his SUV lifted, just before they stopped behind it. "Since you work for me."

"Yes, I do." When they were married, she'd been very young and would have done anything for him. Now she was more mature. Jaded from the way he'd tossed her aside and not so easily swayed. He couldn't always have his way and if she gave in now, he would have the upper hand while they collaborated. It was time to let him know that she wasn't backing down. "My physical presence in Blackwater Lake was not required for me to fulfill my contractual obligation to you."

"Is that so?"

"Absolutely. While I was gone, I put together more decorating options and ideas for you to look over. We can do that right now if you'd like."

He lifted her small suitcase into the cargo compartment, then took her briefcase and stowed it, too. There was a puzzled expression on his face when he met her gaze. "That won't be necessary. Tomorrow is soon enough."

"Okay, then."

Without a word he opened the passenger door for her. Darn him. He always did that.

"Ever the gentleman." She sounded like a shrew but was a sucker for the Galahad routine and had to find a way to fight it off. "You don't have to do that for me."

"I was raised this way."

"By your parents?"

He frowned. "Hastings did insist."

"Well, it makes me uncomfortable." In a way she couldn't explain to him. "Probably because my father was a no-show in my life and I didn't have a male role model."

"A psychologist would have a field day with you."

"No kidding." She thought about it. "Aren't we a pair? I had no father and you had two. Maybe a shrink would give us a group rate."

He laughed. "Always a silver lining."

After shutting her door, he walked around the car and got behind the wheel. "Are you hungry?"

"Why?"

"You are prickly tonight." He started the engine and glanced over. The dashboard lights illuminating his features showed he was smiling. "I have no ulterior motive except that it's the polite thing to do. Manners are something the people who raised me insisted on. Also, I haven't eaten dinner yet. I'm pretty sure my sister's kitchen is closed and stopping somewhere would be faster and easier. And I'd rather not eat alone. How's that for justification?"

"Thorough." She nodded. "Okay. I'm hungry."

"Excellent. I know a place."

Twenty minutes later they were seated at a booth in Bar None. It was a cute, rustic establishment that had buckets of character and charm. Literally. Shelves high on the wall had a grouping of antique items—bucket, washboard, pump and handle, lanterns. The bar that took up the wall opposite of where they sat had a brass foot rail and the plank floor was scratched from wooden chairs sliding over it. The walls were decorated with pictures of cowboys and framed newspaper clippings that looked old and delicate, as if they'd crumble in your hands.

"I like it," she said, after taking in her surroundings.

"It's quiet tonight." He followed her gaze to a couple of guys at the bar. Several of the bistro tables were occupied. "On ladies' night this place really rocks."

"I'm guessing you know this because you were here. Trying to pick someone up." The thought was as annoying as a rock in her shoe even though she had no right to the feeling.

Before he could answer, a very pretty redhead walked over. "Hi, Linc. I didn't expect to see you again so soon. Thought we scared you off."

"Takes more than the three of you to do that. I'm made of sterner stuff."

Three women?

Rose didn't have two fathers, but her single mother had raised her to be polite so an introduction would be good before voicing any of her multiple questions. She stuck out her hand. "We haven't met. I'm Rose Tucker. I work for Linc—his interior-design expert. To decorate his condo." She was rambling and decided to stop right there.

The other woman took her hand and grinned. "Delanie Carlson. It's nice to meet you, Rose. I own Bar None. I work for myself since I own Bar None and inherited it from my father."

"Too much information?" Rose said sheepishly, meaning her own long-winded introduction.

"No." Delanie shrugged. "We'd find out all that stuff anyway. You just saved the town rumor mill a lot of time."

"Happy to help."

Delanie looked at Linc. "To what do I owe a visit from you again so soon?"

"I just picked up Rose from the airport. She had an unexpected trip."

The other woman's gaze sharpened with interest. "Mystery solved."

"Which one would that be?" Rose asked.

"Why he looked lost in here on ladies' night."

Linc made a scoffing sound. "That wasn't lost. I always look like that."

"Really?" The bar owner glanced at Rose, then him. "I don't see it now."

"What do you see?" He asked before Rose could.

"A man who's not sorry his interior-design expert has returned." Delanie shrugged. "Just an opinion and worth what you paid for it."

"Do you see hunger here?" Linc said, pointing at his face. He looked just a little bit uncomfortable at being the subject of this conversation.

"I'm guessing yes?" Delanie said.

"Good answer." Rose liked this woman who was hinting that Linc had missed her. The thought lifted her spirits quite a lot. It shouldn't have. It wasn't a good thing, but there was no denying the truth. "I'm starving. What do you recommend?"

"Do you like hamburgers?" She pulled an order pad from her back jeans pocket.

"I'm all about the fries, but if the burger comes, too, I could manage to choke it down."

"One combo it is then." She laughed.

"Make it two. I'll have a beer. You?" he said to Rose.

"Red wine. Cabernet if you have it."

"I do. Be right back with your drinks, then I'll get those burgers going."

"Thanks."

"I like her," Rose said, watching the woman walk away.

"Yeah. You'd like her friends, too."

"Did you like them?"

"Yes." He shrugged. "Ladies' night is crowded. There was nowhere to sit and they invited me to join them."

"I bet they did." He was an exceptionally good-looking man. Of course women would hit on him.

One of his dark eyebrows quirked up. "You sound a little like a jealous wife."

"And you're acting like a husband with a guilty conscience who's trying to justify carousing."

"Carouse," he said, as if taking the word out for a test drive. "That so isn't what happened. But even if it did, we are legally separated. With a divorce pending."

Pending. Now there was a word.

One that meant the legalities of their split were not carved in stone yet. "Remind me to call your attorney and find out how that's going."

"I'll have him call *you*."

He always one-upped her like that. In spite of the fact that she stood her ground and refused to tell him why she'd left. Maybe because she hadn't explained it to him.

That didn't change anything. She was a girl who was raised to believe she should have a ring on her finger before going to bed with a man. Her current situation proved how deceptively simple that concept was.

Technically she and Linc were still married and sleeping together is what married people were supposed to do. That kiss had reminded her how wonderful sex with Linc had been, but going there now was trouble with a capital *T*. After kissing her he'd brought up Chandler, which told her Linc respected the boundaries of her being in a relationship.

And now she was reminded again why it was so important to keep the breakup with Chandler a secret from Linc. Until the subject of them divorcing came up she'd been thoroughly enjoying her soon-to-be ex-husband. He was handsome and charming and very good company.

It was this charismatic and captivating Linc that she was hiding from. The man who could, with very little effort, coax her into his bed. The same man who hurt her ten years ago and could so easily do it a second time. Losing her heart to Linc again could be too high a price to pay for saving her business.

Chapter Nine

The next day Rose set up her laptop in Linc's condo on a card table he'd borrowed from his sister. She had explained to him that the presentation would be better here in order to help him visualize everything in his space. Using a computer program, she'd done a scaled-down model of each room, but it was small and hard for the average person to envision, hence the field trip.

"Last night I told you I'd been working while I was gone." She glanced up at him. "Prepare to be dazzled."

He was dazzled every time he looked at her. "I can't wait."

The feeling was especially strong right this moment, with the morning sunlight streaming through the window to caress her hair and cheek.

"Linc?" Sitting in one of the two borrowed card-table chairs, she glanced up at him again. "Come around and take a look at the first mock-up. This is the kitchen and family room, where we are now. The furniture is contemporary modern, both sleek and curvy."

Like her, he thought, picturing her in the shower with water turning her skin to—

"The tables are glass," Rose said, interrupting the sensuous thought. "They coordinate with those light fixtures hanging over this bar that separates the two rooms but maintains openness. This area needs definition and that will do it. Plus give you a place for serving food. Or extra seating. Your guests can sit and keep you company while you cook."

"Yeah, that's not going to happen," he said wryly.

"What?" She slid him a look. "You don't visit with people?"

"No. Visiting is my middle name. I don't cook."

"Not my problem." She looked back at the computer screen. "Here's the master bedroom. Going with the same contemporary look, I found a modern take on a four-poster bed."

"It looks like a cage." There were definitely four posts, but made of metal.

"The furniture can change. Just look at the whole concept. With coordinated wall color, comforter, pictures and mirrors it has a chic and sophisticated loft look."

He studied each room as she scrolled through and shook his head. "Gotta say, I'm not loving this."

"Can you be more specific?"

"For starters, it just feels cold and impersonal."

"Changing the wall color can warm it up. A shade with more yellow and gold instead of blue and gray. Can you picture it? Something like we talked about before?"

"Yeah. I don't think that's the problem. It's just too—" He searched for a word and couldn't come up with anything.

"Stark?" she said. "I know what you mean. No wow factor. No pop."

"All of the above," he agreed.

"Okay." She deleted that file. "Let's try something else. Something less…streamlined."

Linc looked carefully at the images as she explained her ideas in detail. Squares and angles for an edgy feel. Geometric with splashes of turquoise, orange and yellow in a lamp here, a wall-hanging there. Or throw pillows.

"Nope," he said, then elaborated. "Just not feelin' it."

"Okay." She nodded thoughtfully. "Let's go through each room and tell me what you don't care for."

He decided to humor her although he could have made it fast.

When the critique was finished, she looked at him with one eyebrow raised. "So, there was nothing about that design you liked?"

"Sorry." He shrugged.

"I really thought you'd like that one."

"If you want me to, I can lie."

"Of course not. You have to be honest. I want you to be happy with the finished product. But this one is a lot like your place in Texas. The bachelor pad you had when we were together."

The one he'd planned to sell or rent. He'd already started looking at houses, a place for them to live and raise a family together. Bitterness at the beautiful, broken dream rolled through him. Since then he'd learned it was better not to have dreams. That way you wouldn't be disappointed.

"It was a lifetime ago," he finally said. "Since then I've—"

"Evolved. Yeah, that's the rumor." She deleted that file. "Okay. Third time's the charm."

"I'm sure it will be a winner," he assured her.

But he was mistaken and gave it thumbs-down.

"What's wrong?" she asked, exasperated but trying to act as if she wasn't.

"Everything is too…fluffy. Too padded. There's a lot of, how should I say this…roundness."

"Really?" She gave him a skeptical look. "I don't think I've ever heard one of my clients describe something that way before."

"Feel free to borrow it anytime," he offered.

She stood and blew out a long breath. "What's going on with you, Linc?"

"I don't know what you mean."

"You're being deliberately narrow-minded."

This was a new side of her, he thought. It was evident last night when he picked her up at the airport and she'd gone toe-to-toe with him and refused to reveal the reason for her trip. And now, he was seeing a toughness about her that was different. He'd once found her innocence intoxicating and he regretted that he'd missed everything that made her who she was now. But this strength was pretty damn sexy.

He folded his arms over his chest. "Narrow-minded? What ever happened to the customer is always right?"

"I get it." She nodded. "Designs are like men. You have to kiss a lot of them to find a winner. But I'm sensing something else is going on here. You're elevating *difficult* to the level of art form."

"How can you say that?"

"Oh, I don't know." She tapped her lip. "Could be your critique, and let me give you examples. Orange isn't the new black, it's only for Halloween and maybe not even then. Glass and chrome make you want to wear sunglasses indoors. And my personal favorite—too much roundness."

"What can I say?"

"Admit you were digging deep to reject everything about these designs."

"In creative endeavors isn't a thick skin required? Is it a little possible that you're being just the tiniest bit sensitive?"

"I'll own up to that if you'll acknowledge that you might be dragging your feet just the tiniest bit," she said, imitating his choice of words.

Her assessment struck a chord but he wouldn't go down easily. "Why would I do that?"

"Exactly what I was wondering. Care to hazard a guess?"

He had one but she wouldn't like it. For that matter he wasn't too happy, either. This presentation coming on the heels of her unexpected trip and his realization that he'd missed her a lot while she was gone had led him to a disconcerting conclusion. He might be looking for excuses to delay and keep her in Blackwater Lake a little longer.

"Nope," he said. "No guesses."

She glared at him. "All I have to say is since you and I have completely different visions of how a living space should look, it's a good thing we're not married."

"It's a technicality," he said, "because we are actually married until the divorce papers are signed."

"Yes. Mason filled me in on the time frame." Whatever he'd said didn't make her look happy. She looked down as if something was going through her mind that she didn't want him to see. "About that—maybe our personal limbo is the problem you're having with decorating this place. It's possible that there's underlying tension, what with the divorce hanging over us."

He could have told her that. His tension was off the charts. He wanted her in his arms, in his bed. That was his grim reality. Visions of touching every square inch of her silky bare skin filled his dreams and made him want the reality. The only thing stopping him was that hitting on her while she was committed to another man would prove Linc actually was as big a jerk as she believed.

"Do you feel tension?" It was an effort to keep his voice neutral, normal.

"No." Her answer came a little too fast. "But if *you* want to terminate our contract and hire someone else, I would completely understand."

"Are you trying to get rid of me?"

"Of course not. I need the work. And the referrals. But I also want you to be happy. And if I'm not the one to do that then you should find someone else. Another decorator. For your home," she added.

"The environment here is important to me, too." But for a different reason. When the contract was fulfilled his debt to her would be satisfied. "And I believe you're the perfect person for the job."

"Okay." She blew out a long breath. "So, it's back to the drawing board. What *do* you want, Linc?"

"Your place." He hadn't planned to say that, but it was true.

"I'm sorry. What?"

"Your apartment. I liked the feel of it. Warm and welcoming." The things in it played a part, but he had a feeling the overall effect had more to do with the fact that she lived in it. That wasn't going to happen here. When this job was done, she was gone.

"Okay, here's what we're going to do." She tapped her lip and seemed to be thinking things over.

"Don't keep me in suspense."

"Most of your...*comments* were about furniture and color choices. So we'll start with furnishings. We'll look at styles on the internet and narrow things down, get a sense of what appeals to you."

She appealed to him but that's not what she meant. "There's a town about an hour from Blackwater Lake. It's bigger and has a furniture store. We can go look."

"Good idea. If you can spare the time."

"I can." And the idea of an outing with her was pretty damned appealing.

Call him a glutton for punishment, but he couldn't resist the temptation to spend time with her while she was there. But if he'd learned anything from the time she'd been gone, it was this. His punishment wasn't having her here. It would start when she left for good.

Linc had been brooding for a couple of days, since his meeting with Rose at the condo and their trip to the furniture store. The plan to throw some work her way, rescue her business and atone for his behavior ten years ago had seemed so simple before. But putting it into practice after kissing her had been complex and problematic. The only easy decision was the one to keep her on. He didn't want anyone else to decorate his condo.

Looking out the big window of his new office, he savored the sight of Black Mountain. It had been named after the town's founding family and beat the heck out of the view of flat landscape that he saw in Dallas. He had a good feeling about relocating here and hoped his rosy outlook, no pun intended, didn't change when Rose left.

After spending time with her, the prospect of this town without her in it wasn't quite as cheerful. It was entirely possible he'd subconsciously sabotaged her presentation as a delaying tactic. Identifying the problem was half the battle so he would work on being more cooperative.

He'd brought the borrowed card table and chairs to his

newly leased office space and would keep it until the furniture arrived in a couple of days. This retail center built by Burke and Sloan Holden was ninety percent occupied and located a couple miles from their hotel project nearing completion.

Linc had plans with his brother-in-law for several new housing developments and multiple neighborhoods with graduated price points. There would be a population increase following all the new construction in the area and the expanded workforce would need housing.

He was setting up his laptop on the card table when the office door opened. He smiled when the familiar figure walked in. "Well, if it isn't Sam Hart."

"Hey, Linc. Alex said I'd find you here."

"And why were you looking for me?"

"To say hello."

He knew Sam was very soon relocating the Hart financial corporate offices to Blackwater Lake and was here to check on the building. But he had a feeling the move was more than a business decision. "Ellie got to you, too."

"About this town being the best place in the whole world?" There was a twinkle in the other man's eyes. "Maybe. But I'll deny it if you tell her that."

"Me? Betray a brother's trust? As far as I'm concerned it's strictly business." Linc shook his head. But he felt a small twinge of regret. He'd meant "brother" in the sense of male solidarity because you couldn't have it both ways. Either you were a Hart and part of the inner circle or you weren't. He wasn't. "How does the rest of the family feel about this move?"

"You know Mom. There's drama before she gives her blessing to, and I quote, 'whatever will make you happy.'"

"And moving away from Dallas will do that for you?"

"Any place where my ex-wife didn't try to drag out our

divorce and, not only do her damnedest to clean me out but get her hooks into Hart Industries, too, has got to be an improvement."

"That was a hard time for you."

"*Hard?* Such a small, insignificant word to describe the hell that woman put me through." Sam shook his head. "Never again."

"What did Hastings say about branching out?"

"You mean Dad?"

"*Your* dad, not mine."

Not for the first time since learning the truth, Linc studied his half brother. His own height was six feet, but Sam was a couple of inches taller and his hair was quite a bit darker. They both had blue eyes, but Linc's were a different shade. Ellie, Sam and Cal all had their father's chin, but Linc's came from a stranger his mother had slept with. A man who had stooped to taking advantage of a vulnerable woman.

"Dad thinks the expansion is a good way to grow the company and told *our* Mom that Blackwater Lake isn't on another planet." Sam sighed. "I'll be commuting for a few weeks while the finishing touches are completed. The house I'm building here is nearly finished, too."

"You're building? Ellie didn't mention that."

"Shocking lack of transparency since she's the architect and Alex is the building contractor."

"That doesn't surprise me as much as Ellie missing an opportunity to share news and gossip." Although, to be fair, their sister had been preoccupied with the fact that Linc had been married and she didn't know.

"Speaking of gossip and news…" Sam folded his arms over his chest. "She told me about you and Rose."

"What exactly did she say?" Linc had known this would

happen, but didn't want to reveal more detail than his sister already had.

"That you had the shortest marriage in Hart family history. Even more brief than our own infamous Uncle Foster's union with what's-her-name."

"Again. Hastings's brother is your uncle, not mine."

"Doesn't matter who claims him. He's had a colorful and checkered past where women are concerned."

"I'm not a Hart."

Sam held up a hand. "That so isn't where I was going with this."

"I probably don't want to hear that, either."

"Don't care what you want." Sam shrugged. "And I'd put odds on the fact that you're not going to want to hear this, but tough. According to our sister, who, rumor has it, is very good at observing and making accurate assumptions about these things, there is still something going on between you and Rose. Even after all this time."

Linc snorted. "Ellie is a romantic and sees what she wants to see. If you will, through rose-colored glasses. Pardon the pun."

"Look, she told me why you ended the marriage. Also that you screwed up the divorce."

"She'll never let me live that down," Linc grumbled.

"She's not the only one. But that's not my point. I get it, Linc. Why you went into a tailspin after finding out who your dad is. Ellie doesn't understand why you can't shrug it off, join hands with everyone and sing 'Kumbaya,' but I can see how getting information like that would destroy a guy's whole foundation."

"Good." He was glad someone was on Team Linc. "Then you know why Rose is off-limits."

"If you really feel that way, why is she here to decorate your condo?"

Linc explained about her failing business and his intention to make amends by giving her a hand. "So you can understand that other than a business boost, there can't be anything personal between us."

"Actually, I really don't get it."

"Seriously?"

"Yeah." Sam slid his fingertips into the front pockets of his slacks. "It's been ten years, there's still a spark and you're not divorced. Seems like a whole lot of check marks in the 'second chance' column to me."

"After your less than successful romantic track record, do you really think you're the best one to give me advice?" Linc let that sink in, then added, "There isn't anything between Rose and me and there never can be because my situation hasn't changed."

"Sure it has. You've had a lot of years to get over the shock. A lot of years to get over *her*. And if Ellie is right about her power to sniff out the chemistry between you and Rose, it's something you should explore."

"So says the man who vows never again," Linc reminded him.

"We're talking about you, not me." Sam didn't look the least bit offended.

"Did Ellie send you to talk to me?"

"That's classified."

"I'm going to take that as a yes." This was damned irritating. He was having a hard enough time keeping his hands off Rose as it was. He didn't need his older brother, the one he'd always looked up to, giving his blessing to push the envelope. "And since when are you my fairy godmother? Or, for that matter, do what Ellie tells you to do?"

"Since always, little brother. Don't you? At least I'm sensitive. I thought it best to have this, we're on a pun roll,

Hart-to-Hart here at your office, where it's just the two of us. Man-to-man."

Linc figured it was a waste of energy to remind him yet again that he wasn't a Hart. In spite of his irritation, the blatant admission regarding his motivation drew a reluctant smile from Linc. "I try not to let Ellie know how much power she has."

"Good luck with that, little brother."

"I know." Linc dragged his fingers through his hair. "But there are two reasons why our sister is wrong about this."

"And what might those be?" Sam asked.

"Rose is involved with a man. I don't cross that line."

His brother frowned. "It's not crossing a line if you just tell her how you feel. So, I repeat, if you still have feelings for her put them out there."

"I can't."

"Why not?"

"Nothing has changed. I'm still not a Hart. When we got married she thought I was. She thought she knew what she was getting, but she didn't."

"She knows now what happened, so does it really matter anymore?"

"It does to me." Linc started pacing and there was a lot of room to do it since the space was nearly empty. He needed a lot of area because the intensity pouring through him was big. "I don't know who I am."

"Do you even realize what a ridiculous, archaic attitude that is?"

"That's easy for you to say since you're not the one who's a bastard," Linc retorted. "You're completely secure in your DNA."

"You are the same person I grew up with," Sam protested. "The same brother and son you always were."

"No." Linc shook his head. "Now half of me is a mystery."

"Okay," Sam agreed. "Whose fault is that?"

"Off the top of my head, I'd say it's our mother's fault, along with the man who seduced her."

"Not what I meant. Find out about your DNA. Fill in the blanks."

"What are you suggesting?"

"If the unknown is what's holding you back, change it. Get to know your biological father."

Linc stopped pacing and met his brother's gaze. "What if he's a jerk who takes advantage of women?"

"That's his problem, not yours. It's not what you do."

"I did it to Rose ten years ago. I walked out on her. And he did it to our mother. I researched him. He's been married four times and divorced three."

"Poor bastard," Sam said.

"What if I inherited the jerk factor from him?"

"First of all the two situations are completely different." When Linc opened his mouth to protest, Sam held up a hand to stop him. "Trust me. Think about it. You'll figure out how they're not the same. And second, listen to yourself. Do you know how stupid it sounds? You're a good man."

"Easy for you to say."

"Probably. But just as easy for you to put your questions to rest. As far as I know you only saw him that one time, when he told you who he was."

"Just the once," Linc confirmed. He hadn't wanted anything to do with the guy.

"So, reach out. Get to know him, what he's like. Do it for yourself and let go of the ghosts."

Linc nodded. "I'll think about it."

"Good. I expected you to tell me to go to hell," Sam admitted.

"Don't think I didn't consider that." Linc smiled.

There was a spark of the devil in his brother's blue eyes when he said, "I'm looking forward to meeting Rose."

"Don't tell me. You're coming to dinner."

"Ellie invited me." Sam shrugged.

"Maybe she'll come to her senses and uninvite you between now and then."

"Don't count on it, bro."

If Linc counted on anything now it was his brothers and sister. After the big reveal ten years ago he'd thought of his siblings in terms of half, but that was about him, not them. He was the one with a different father but Sam was right. They had grown up together and Linc was glad Sam, Cal and Ellie were still in his life and treated him no differently. He was the one who'd changed and, again, it could be possible that Sam was right. Maybe it was time Linc faced the man who was responsible for ruining his life.

But whatever he found out wouldn't change the situation with Rose. He wouldn't cross the line into personal territory and risk hurting her again. Somehow he had to find the strength to keep from kissing her a second time.

Chapter Ten

Rose was working in the McKnights' home office and deeply involved in coming up with a decorating theme that would impress Linc. Since his negative critique of what she thought of as some of her best work, she really didn't understand why he wanted to keep her on. Anyone else would have fired her. Since he didn't, she was determined to wow him.

He'd said he liked her place so that gave her a starting point, but nothing in it was expensive. Everything had come from thrift stores, antique shops and garage sales because her budget was thinner than a high-fashion supermodel. So she was going to decorate Linc's condo the way she would have done her space if she'd had money.

She completely lost track of everything and tuned out the distant sounds of doors closing and hushed voices. Then there was an unmistakable squeal of happiness from Ellie. Rose glanced at her phone and noted that it was closing in on dinnertime. She should probably come out of the cave. If she was being honest, burying herself in work could have been a coping mechanism, better known as hiding from Linc.

The intense way he looked at her did funny things to her insides, not unlike the way he'd made her feel when she first knew him. Before he broke her heart. She was older and wiser now so why would this be happening to her again? If it was just Linc, she would stay put and not come out, but his sister was involved. Ellie and her husband had been nothing but incredibly gracious. They deserved friendliness in return.

Rose shut down everything and walked into the kitchen. The usual suspects were there—Ellie with Leah in her arms. Alex and Linc. And then there was a very good-looking man she vaguely remembered from working at Hart Industries ten years ago.

"Rose, there you are." Ellie shifted a squirmy Leah onto her hip. "I thought we were going to have to send search-and-rescue to find you."

"Sorry. I got caught up in work." She gave Linc a look that said it was all his fault and hoped he got the message. "It's hard to deal with a client who doesn't like anything."

"So, this is Rose." The good-looking man studied her as if he'd never seen her before.

"Guilty." She figured he wouldn't have noticed her ten years ago because a lot of people worked for the company and she was pretty far down the food chain. Her heart fluttered when she glanced at Linc and realized he'd noticed her.

"I'm Sam Hart, brother of Ellie and Linc. Brother-in-law of Alex and uncle of Leah."

"Nice to meet you." She shook his hand. "Rose Tucker,

interior-design expert of Linc and annoying houseguest to the extraordinarily gracious Ellie and Alex."

"I wish Cal was here," Ellie said. "It would be a family reunion."

"In case you're not aware," Sam said to Rose, "Calhoun Hart is our brother. He's in the middle, between Linc and me."

"In charge of the energy research-and-development branch of Hart Industries," his sister explained. "And it would take an act of God to pry him out of his office."

"Why?" She didn't recall ever seeing the elusive Cal Hart when she'd been employed at Hart Industries.

"He's a notorious workaholic." Sam slid his fingers into the pockets of his slacks. The long sleeves of his white dress shirt were rolled to midforearm and his red silk tie was loosened, giving him a carelessly dashing look. "I'm worried about him."

"Me, too," his sister agreed.

"Why?" Rose asked again.

"He hasn't taken a vacation in years. If ever," Sam explained.

"I'm thinking of holding a family intervention." Ellie absently kissed her daughter's soft cheek. "He's going to burn out and that won't be pretty."

"True." Sam stared at his brother. "Look what happened to Linc. He's exhibit A."

"I have no idea what you're talking about," he said. "There was nothing to see."

"Because you went all lone wolf and radio silent," Sam retorted. "After the family secret was spilled you fell off the grid. For how long?"

"Two years," Ellie said.

Linc took the beer his brother-in-law handed him. "I

don't suppose there's any way the two of you are going to let this drop?"

Sam looked at Ellie and they both said, "Not a chance."

"That's what I thought. So," he said, looking at the watch on his wrist, "how about I give you five minutes to rag on me. Get creative. Give it your best shot. Then we never have to speak of it again."

Rose watched brother and sister think that over. There was a part of her still wanting to see Linc suffer a little for what he'd done. "Is it just me, or does having permission to annoy him without mercy take all the fun out of it?"

"Ah, so you're piling on," Linc said. "How about you, Alex? Feel free to sink to their level. I can take it."

His brother-in-law laughed. "Appreciate the invitation, but I'm handing out drinks. I'll just line yours up, partner. You're going to need them."

"Excellent," Linc said.

"It's kind of a brilliant strategy when you think about it," Rose said. "A time limit on teasing."

"Thank you." Linc's tone was a little smug.

"I don't think it was a compliment." Sam studied his brother. "And who can blame your soon-to-be ex-wife. Yeah, Ellie told me you have the sensitivity of a water buffalo."

"I didn't say that," Ellie protested.

"I filled in the blanks. Probably more efficiently than Linc handled the divorce." There was a wicked, teasing look in the man's eyes.

Rose hadn't been sure what to expect from this guy whose loyalty would be to his family, but he was *not* putting a serious spin on the situation. And bless him for taking the awkwardness out of it. The best way to deal with the elephant in the room was to confront it directly and make fun.

"I think I like you, Sam Hart," Rose said. "And yes, this time it will be a full-service dissolution of marriage."

"You might want to rethink the divorce, little brother." The oldest Hart sibling had a thoughtful expression on his face. "Your wife is as smart as she is pretty. Has it ever occurred to her that she's working for a complete idiot? We already knew that after his disappearance. I used to call him the missing Linc."

"Three minutes and counting," Linc said after a glance at his watch.

"Don't you wonder how he kept Rose a secret from us at all?" Ellie asked.

Sam took the beer Alex handed over. "If I met someone as pretty as Rose, I'd have kept her to myself, too."

"No one asked you," Linc snapped.

"Actually, Ellie did," Sam pointed out.

Ellie set down her daughter and the child toddled to the family room toybox. Obviously she was bored with this grown-up talk. Rose, on the other hand, was kind of liking the sibling interaction.

Sam took a sip of his beer, then said, "I never knew you two were dating, never mind the quickie wedding."

"One minute left." Linc met her gaze and there was an apology in his.

"It's interesting to watch the dynamic between all of you," Rose said. "I'm an only child and would have given anything to have a big brother."

"Want mine?" Ellie set corn chips and guacamole on the kitchen island. "I just can't believe I didn't know Linc was serious enough about anyone to get married. Then he disappeared."

Rose understood the sentiment. After all, the love of her life left her with very little explanation. Now she had one and knew Linc had been betrayed in a more profound and basic way than any of them.

"You know, since I found out what Linc was going through right after we got married, I've tried to put myself in his shoes. How would I feel if I found out the man I thought was my father…wasn't." Rose shrugged. "I can't even imagine what I would do in that situation."

"Thank you, Rose." Linc's mouth turned up at the corners. "I appreciate you sticking up for me."

"It wasn't for you," she teased. "I'd have done the same for anyone."

"You're sweeter to him than he deserves. She's also right." Ellie looked at Sam.

"It pains me to say it, but he did have the right to get weird." Sam grinned. "But he's still our brother and we love him. That gives us the right to rag on him relentlessly. It's our way of keeping him from turning into an eccentric recluse."

"So," Linc said. "You're picking on me out of love."

"Exactly," Sam agreed.

"I just got a warm fuzzy," Linc said wryly.

"Now that we've cleared it all up let me continue—"

"Time is up." Linc looked at Sam. "I think we've exhausted the subject. If you care nothing for me, just take pity on Rose. It's entirely possible she doesn't want to rehash this whole dark past."

"I agree," Ellie chimed in.

"You're my baby sister," Sam said. "We don't have to do what you say."

"You do in my house. And I've got backup." She smiled at her muscular husband.

"Just call me the enforcer," Alex said drily. He dipped a chip in the guacamole and ate it.

Rose watched the siblings continue to banter and saw

for herself the love and affection Linc had from his family. She sensed they'd teased him since childhood and were treating him no differently since learning they didn't share a father.

He was the one with the chip on his shoulder. And she felt a great deal of sympathy for him. The past really had a grip and wouldn't let go. The empathy was far different from what she'd experienced when he'd shown up out of the blue at her door.

Obviously knowing the facts of what happened had helped her to get to this place, but that wasn't the only thing.

She was afraid that hot kiss had started melting the ice around her heart.

The next morning Linc was showered, shaved and dressed. He stood in the bathroom he shared with Rose and stared hard at the door to her room. He needed coffee almost as much as he needed a woman and right now his odds of getting a cup of caffeine seemed the best. Something hot would be good after another cold shower. The thought of Rose in the bed just a few steps away never failed to make his body tight and tense. No way was he going to have her, so he headed downstairs and found the kitchen empty and the house unusually quiet.

"Weird," he said to himself.

He was used to the sounds of his niece giggling, crying or squealing with delight over something wondrous to a child. Sometimes he heard his sister laughing in that certain way she did when her husband was getting frisky. They were happy family sounds, the kind that were unlikely to be heard in his condo.

His biological father got marriage wrong three times and Linc had a failure on his own record. That was enough to keep him from another mistake. But staying here with Ellie and watching her so happy with her own family made him envious of being a Hart in name only.

"Enough with the downer attitude." He sighed. "And stop talking to yourself. The neighbors are starting to talk."

He walked directly to the coffeemaker, where he found a note from his sister. It read:

Dear Linc,
Alex and I had early appointments. Help yourself to anything. Coffee's ready to go. Just turn it on. I'm confident you can handle that. If there's nothing in my house to eat that appeals to you…starve. Or take Rose to the Harvest Café. It's awesome. See you at dinner. Love, Your favorite sister.

He turned on the coffeemaker and said, "Bless you, Ellie."

The machine started doing its thing and he heard the shower go on upstairs, telling him that his decorator would be ready for breakfast shortly. So, he checked out the contents of the refrigerator. Eggs, cheese, mushrooms and tomatoes would make an omelet. There was cut-up cantaloupe and English muffins. That all worked for him so he sliced the ingredients and readied pots, pans and utensils for cooking. The coffee was ready and he got out two mugs, then poured some of the hot black liquid in one of them and waited.

Moments later Rose walked into the kitchen. What was it about this particular woman that hit him like a sucker punch to the gut every time he saw her? She had on a white T-shirt and worn jeans that were just tight enough to show off her curvy little body. It was enough to make a man break out in a cold sweat. Her shiny dark hair was carelessly pulled back into a ponytail with wisps caressing her face. If she had on makeup he couldn't tell and it didn't matter. She was still the most beautiful woman he'd ever seen.

She glanced around and suddenly looked wary at the prospect of them being alone. "Where's Ellie?"

"Early appointment." He held up the note. "We have been abandoned and must fend for ourselves.

"Looks like she got everything ready." Rose indicated the preparations underway.

Linc nodded. "Oh, that. All me."

"You're cooking?"

"Don't sound so surprised. I've got skills."

"That's not breaking news," she said. "But I wasn't aware that cooking was one of them."

"There's a lot about me you don't know."

"You're right about that." Her full lips pulled tight for a moment.

As soon as those words were out of his mouth he wanted them back. No one needed a reminder that their short marriage hadn't given him time to find out what would have her laughing in that special way when he got playful. Or to learn all the particular places to touch her and make her cry out with pleasure. He wanted to now and had only himself to blame for that dead end. Time for damage control. He'd had plenty of experience learning about *that*.

"Coffee?" he asked.

"I thought you'd never ask."

"Coming right up." He poured some into the second mug, then fixed it her way and set it in front of her on the island. "The breakfast menu is mushroom, tomato and cheese omelets. I hope that meets with your approval."

There was a vindictive expression in her eyes when she said, "I don't know. I'm not lovin' it. Cold and impersonal.

No wow factor. No pop. Just not feelin' it. Too mushroomy. A lot of roundness. And cheesy."

"Cute." He couldn't help smiling as he stared across the granite-topped counter. "Is it customary for you to punish a client when he or she doesn't approve of your creative ideas?"

"Of course not. That's no way to do business. You're the only one who gets that special treatment."

"Lucky me." If he'd wanted an interior designer without personal baggage he'd have hired a perfect stranger. "So, are you hungry enough to take a chance that I won't give you food poisoning?"

"Normally I'm not a fan of living dangerously but I'll make an exception. Mostly because it looks like you did a nice job cutting up those mushrooms without taking off a finger."

"Okay, then. Prepare to be amazed."

"With you I'm always prepared."

Linc was pretty sure she wasn't referring to his culinary ability, but decided not to make an issue of it. There were hills to die on and this wasn't one of them. All part of the penance package.

It didn't take long until the mushrooms and tomatoes were ready for the egg mixture and cheese. When the muffins were toasted and buttered, they filled plates, then sat at the circular oak table in the nook.

Rose smiled when she looked at the table. "Did you tell Ellie this has too much roundness?"

"Have you met my sister?" He shook his head. "No way."

She laughed and then took a bite of the eggs. "This is really good."

"I'm glad you like it." He liked watching her enjoy it.

They ate in silence for a few moments as he searched

for a topic of discussion that wasn't about food poisoning, severing fingers or anything else that could land him in deep doo-doo. "Thanks for having my back last night. I know you tried to stick up for me when Ellie and Sam were giving me a hard time."

"Don't mention it. Guess I'm a sucker for the underdog."

"A softie." It had surprised the heck out of him when she came to his defense. He expected her to pile on and wouldn't have blamed her if she did. "Just wanted you to know I noticed and appreciated."

"You're welcome. I'd have done the same for anyone."

Anyone she used to be married to? Or any guy she once had a soft spot for? Speaking of guys… "How's Chandler? Have you heard from him?"

"No." All of a sudden she was so intent on her omelet that she wouldn't look up. She just concentrated on moving the food around her plate.

"Is it unusual for you to go a while without talking?"

"We understand each other if that's what you're asking."

Actually it wasn't and she hadn't answered the question. Besides not making eye contact, she now looked as if she was the kind of designer who used substandard materials and charged the client for top-of-the-line things. And got caught.

"What's going on, Rose?"

"I don't know what you mean."

"You're a terrible liar. For what it's worth, that's a quality I admire since I was lied to for most of my life. But there's something you're not telling me. Something about you and Chandler." He hadn't pushed her much about the motivation behind her trip. But a thought occurred to him and the idea made him want to put his fist through a wall. "When you were gone… Did you go to Vegas and marry Chandler?"

That got her to look at him and her jaw dropped. "No!"

He was relieved to hear that. "Then what's going on? And don't say nothing."

She put her fork down and pushed the plate away with half the omelet uneaten. "If you must know, I did go to see Chandler."

"Booty call?" Again those were words he wanted back. But not as much as he wanted to know the answer.

"No."

"Then why?"

"Has anyone ever told you you're irritatingly persistent? Since you won't let it go, I broke up with him." There was annoyance in her tone but not hurt.

Before he did a triumphant arm pump he wanted to be sure he'd heard right. "So that's where you went? To break up with him in person?"

"Yes."

Right after they'd kissed. There had to be a connection and he would bet everything he had it was because that kiss had meant something to her. But she'd been back for a while now and hadn't said a word about this. Why?

"Were you ever going to tell me?"

"You're not entitled to details of my personal life." There was a defensive note in her voice. "Why would I tell you?"

Because the kiss had meant something to him and he wanted to know if he was the only one. "It feels as if you're keeping it a secret. And you don't have to. Not from me."

She toyed with the handle of her coffee mug. "You're the last person I wanted to share this information with."

"Why? You were very happy to share the fact that you and Chandler were moving in the matrimony direction." He met her gaze. "And then we kissed."

She blew out a long breath. "The fact is that I don't trust

you, Linc. That hasn't changed. I thought I made myself clear on the subject."

"Haven't we gotten past that?"

"Look, I believe you're sorry about what happened. But then—"

"What?"

"Like you said. There was that kiss." Her eyes darkened with doubt. For herself? Or him?

"And?" he persisted. "I dare you to say it didn't mean anything. I know differently. And you broke things off with him."

"Like you said. I can't lie. The kiss was nice," she admitted.

"But?" God, he hated that word.

"I can't forget that you betrayed me once and distrusting you is the best defense I have against it happening again."

He wanted to put his fist through a wall and this time it had nothing to do with Chandler. This was all about him. "Rose, I would never deliberately hurt you."

"I know. Not deliberately. I get that. You might not mean to but it could happen."

"So you're not willing to take a risk? Even though you enjoyed it as much as I did?"

"I like chili cheese fries, too, but that doesn't mean they're good for me. Besides, you and I want different things. Let's just leave it at that." She stood up and took her plate to the sink. "I have work to do."

Linc sat there for a long time thinking about what she'd just said. On the upside, she and Chandler were over. Also on the upside, regarding her reaffirmation that she didn't trust him, she'd only said let's leave it at that. A far cry from slamming the door in his face.

And yet, of all the things she could have said to tick him off, not trusting him was by far the winner. He wanted more from her—exactly what, he wasn't sure. And it didn't really matter because there wasn't a chance in hell of more ever happening. But there was a chance of earning back her faith in him. He promised himself that when her work in Blackwater Lake was done she would damn well trust him again.

He was going to make that happen or die trying.

Chapter Eleven

It was a thrift-store kind of day.

After her talk with Linc over the breakfast he'd cooked, Rose had practically barricaded herself in the office and worked on the computer until her eyes ached. It was time to treat herself and get some fresh air, somewhere away from the tantalizingly masculine and intoxicatingly tempting scent of that man. Linc was going to be with Alex all day and left the car for her. She loved poking through second-hand stores and there was one in Blackwater Lake. That's where she was headed.

If only she could head her thoughts away from Linc. The man defied rational thought, at least for her. He'd seemed happy about her breakup with Chandler and that made her nervous. When she got nervous she pushed back. Hence her bringing up the trust issue again when she no longer believed that he'd married her just to get what he wanted. But that didn't mean the pain of it was canceled out. Putting her heart in his hands wasn't a smart move.

Since she'd furnished her own apartment from the thrift store she wanted to see what she could find for him. After pulling into the parking lot, she found a space, then exited the car.

The large building was painted barn-red and had white trim. Probably in another life it had been a barn, but now there was a lot to look at by the big, double-wide entrance doors. Half barrels used as flowerpots dripped with pink, purple, red and yellow blooms. A big, old wagon wheel was propped up against the outside wall. Motivational sayings painted on pieces of metal were hanging there. The Best Antiques Are Old Friends. Live, Love, Laugh. Home Is Where the Heart Is.

"Wonder if Linc would like that," she mumbled, looking things over.

"What was that?"

Rose hadn't noticed anyone standing there and now saw an older woman with short blond hair wearing a denim shirt with the thrift-store logo on it. "Sorry. I was just talking to myself."

"I've never done that before," the woman teased. "My husband, Brewster, says it's because I like to hear myself talk." She held out her hand. "Agnes Smith. Folks call me Aggie."

"Nice to meet you. Rose Tucker," she said, shaking the other woman's hand.

"You're new in town." It wasn't a question.

"I'm not a permanent resident. Just here for a job."

"What is it you do?" the older woman asked.

"I'm an interior designer. Lincoln Hart hired me to decorate his new condominium."

"I hear the units in that complex up by Black Mountain are pretty fancy."

"It's a wonderful floor plan. Well thought out and lots of

square footage. Not so fancy yet, though." Rose shrugged. "It needs paint, cupboards, countertops, flooring and fixtures. And that's before furnishings."

Aggie glanced over her shoulder at the shadowy interior of the store filled with things people no longer had a use for. "Can't imagine what you're doing here then. Seems to me you're in the wrong place. Jumping the gun, you might say."

"I'm actually looking for inspiration. Trying to get ideas. And I think Linc is an old soul."

"Haven't met the man yet, so I couldn't say. But looking doesn't cost anything except time. If you'll excuse me, I'm expecting a truck that was picking up donations. It's my job to figure out what to do with it all."

"Of course. Nice to meet you, Aggie."

"Likewise." The older woman smiled, then headed toward what was probably the back of the building.

Rose decided to start on the first aisle and do a quick overview of what was there, making notes for anything worth another look. After checking out two thirds of the inventory, she concluded a lot of it fell into the category of "one man's trash is another man's treasure." But there were quite a few pieces of glassware that were noteworthy and might just interest collectors. She liked a couple of pictures of the lake and mountains, and since Linc approved of her taste, he might like them, too.

The final third of the store was furniture—dining room tables and chairs, some matching, some not so much. China cabinets, dressers and vanities. A pretty young woman with strawberry-blond hair and brown eyes was intently studying a twin-sized brass headboard.

Rose took a long look at the graceful lines and delicate detail. "That's really a nice piece."

"I thought so, too." The woman gave her a friendly

smile. "I promised my little girl a pretty bed. Maybe for Christmas."

Rose studied the headboard a little more. "How old is she?"

"Eight. I've been tucking away whatever extra cash I can that doesn't go back into my business."

"I'm a business owner, too, so believe me, I understand. What do you do?"

"A florist. My aunt left the shop on Main Street to me. Every Bloomin' Thing. I'm Faith Connelly, by the way."

"Rose Tucker. For what it's worth, I think your daughter…"

"Phoebe," she said.

"Phoebe… Adorable name. She'll love it."

"I think so, too. And I can kill two birds with one stone. Maybe that's nothing more than justification for the expenditure but the money the thrift store makes goes to the Sunshine Fund."

"I saw the sign outside that said all proceeds go to the fund," Rose said. "What is it?"

"A Blackwater Lake thing." Faith smiled and there was a lot of civic pride in her expression. "Mayor Goodwin-McKnight started it to give a helping hand to anyone down on their luck. People donate used items to the thrift store but cash is also gratefully accepted. And there are potluck fund-raising events, usually scheduled around a holiday like Halloween, Thanksgiving or Christmas. Or any other occasion the mayor can come up with for a party."

"That's very cool." Rose knew how it felt to be down on her luck. Her mom could have used help more than once and if working for Linc didn't jump-start her business Rose wasn't sure that *she* wouldn't need a boost from an organization like the Sunshine Fund.

"Yeah, it is. Community spirit here in this town is something special." The young woman smiled. "Speaking of community spirit, I forgot to ask. I haven't heard about a new business opening up here. What do you do?"

"Oh, mine isn't actually here. I'm from Texas. I was hired for a job in Blackwater Lake." And the promise of more work, she thought, mentally crossing her fingers. "I'm an interior designer."

"Do you work for *the* Lincoln Hart?" Faith's warm brown eyes grew very wide.

"Yes. Although I don't think there's more than one. The world isn't ready for two of him." A single Linc was more than she could handle. "How did you know?"

"I put two and two together. People in town are talking about him buying that condo at the base of the mountain and bringing his own interior designer from Dallas." Faith shrugged. "Being honest, the people doing the talking are women."

"Ah." Rose was surprised that her feelings about this information were decidedly *not* neutral.

"I haven't met him yet, so maybe he's not a flower-buying kind of guy."

"He used to be."

"What was that?" the other woman asked.

"Hmm? Oh, nothing." The memory rushed back so strong it threw Rose off balance. Ten years ago, almost every time she saw him, he brought her flowers—everything from a single rose to bouquets so big she could barely get her arms around them. "So he's not a flower buyer?"

"Since I haven't met him yet, I'd have to say no. But others have. He and Alex McKnight are business partners, but you probably already know that."

"Yes." She confirmed the information because it was obviously common knowledge. Normally she didn't talk about clients because it wasn't professional. A reputation for loose lips could kill a business like hers. There was that trust issue again.

"Is he as good-looking as I've heard?"

"Well, that's hard to say." Rose wanted to fan herself every time he walked into a room, but revealing that would be indiscreet. "Beauty is in the eye of the beholder, as they say."

"True." Faith nodded thoughtfully. "Also true is the fact that single women in Blackwater Lake are quivering with excitement at having a wealthy bachelor take up residence in our little corner of Montana. A man who, rumor says, is not hard on the eyes."

"Are you single?" The information about women made Rose a little tense. That was her best explanation for that question popping out of her mouth.

"Yes." Faith frowned. "I mean no. Actually let me re-phrase in a more coherent sentence. I'm not married. Di-vorced, to put a finer point on it. And considering my horrible history with men, well... To mangle a quote from Scarlett O'Hara and *Gone with the Wind*, 'as God is my witness, I'll never fall in love again.'"

Not that she wished a bad relationship on anyone, but Rose relaxed. "Seems to me there's also a song with a similar theme."

"It's my motto and I'm sticking to it," Faith vowed. "But other ladies in this town have different ideas and they all include your Lincoln Hart."

"He's not mine, actually." Although he kind of was until the divorce was done. "And he's no doubt used to all the attention."

"Probably so if the rumors about money and looks are true. But someone said they Googled him and couldn't find anything about his dating history. He's either very discreet or gay."

Rose knew for a fact that the latter wasn't true and she couldn't deny a sliver of satisfaction that he couldn't be connected to one special woman. "I have nothing to share."

"That's okay. I understand. And I'm sure there's more than one determined woman in this town who will use her assets to unlock his secrets." Faith looked at her watch. "Shoot, I have to get going. And I need to see if Aggie will hold this for me if I leave a deposit." She took the tag on the headboard. "Enjoy your stay in Blackwater Lake. I really enjoyed talking to you."

Rose mumbled something appropriate because her mind was racing. She liked Faith and it was nice talking to her, except for the part about women looking to hook up with Linc. It bothered her and she realized two things simultaneously. Her anger toward him was gone and she couldn't hide behind it any more. The second thing was even more troubling.

The idea of women throwing themselves at Linc and him catching them was deeply disturbing. That was the classic definition of jealousy. A prerequisite for that feeling was caring about someone.

That meant she cared about Linc. Now what was she going to do? She had to get this job moving faster and herself out of Blackwater Lake before there was hell to pay.

"Tell me again why we're here."

The "here" in Rose's question was the Harvest Café and Linc had brought her as part of his trust offensive. "You've been working very hard on my behalf and I'm not easy."

"That's not breaking news." The words were mocking but her mouth turned up at the corners.

"I just wanted to say thank you for putting up with me. Dinner is my way of doing that."

They were standing by the Please Wait to be Seated

sign in the restaurant on Main Street in Blackwater Lake. It was a weeknight and the place was crowded. Although Linc had one, a person didn't need a master's degree in business to see that this eating establishment was successful. The summer tourist season was just around the corner and it was likely to be even more hectic in here.

Rose looked up at him, a question in her eyes. "Ellie told you to take me to dinner, didn't she?"

"No." Her dubious attitude didn't bother him. She would see he was a man of his word. A regular Boy Scout. "When I mentioned to her that I wanted to do this for my patient and creative decorator she said she had no idea that I was so sensitive to another person's needs."

"Go, Ellie." Rose laughed.

"So, relax. Stand down. I have no ulterior motive." Other than to win her trust.

A pretty brunette carrying menus walked up to them. She was wearing a name tag that read Maggie.

"Table for two?"

"Yes."

"Right this way. Follow me."

Linc put his hand to the small of Rose's back. The gesture was automatic, some would call it gentlemanly. Both might be true. For him it was an excuse to touch her. The downside was that he wanted to do so much more.

In an intimate corner of the restaurant Maggie stopped by a secluded table. "Is this all right?"

"Great. It's the one I'd have chosen," he said. "But tell me, where would you have seated us if it wasn't okay? The place is full."

"That's a good question. And the answer would depend on how hungry you are because a wait would be involved." The woman smiled, clearly understanding that he was teasing.

"From my experience that means the food would be worth waiting for," he said.

"It is. And I'm not just saying that because I'm the co-owner." She studied them. "I don't think I've seen you in here before."

"Because we haven't been," Rose said. "I'm Rose Tucker."

Maggie nodded. "The interior designer."

"Yes. How did you know?"

"Apparently you were in the thrift store the other day. Aggie Smith came in for dinner with her husband and I saw Faith Connelly in the grocery store."

"I heard that people talk," Rose said, "but didn't expect it to get around so fast."

"It's what happens when you ask someone what's new," the woman explained. "I'm Maggie Potter by the way."

"Lincoln Hart." He shook the woman's hand.

"Welcome to my humble establishment. I hope you enjoy your dinner."

"Thanks." He held Rose's chair while she sat, then took the one across from her.

"We don't see manners like that in here every day," Maggie commented. "Not that our clientele runs to the Neanderthal variety. But that was impressive, Mr. Hart."

"Linc."

"Just saying…" Maggie smiled at them, then walked away.

When they were alone Rose said, "This isn't a date."

"I'm aware."

"Then why did you hold my chair?"

"It's what a guy does."

"Not really," she responded. "I know of no guys who do that."

"Then you're hanging out with the wrong guys. It's the

way I was raised." He sighed. "Really, Rose, you should set the bar higher."

"Speaking of bars… Unless you want women following you around and throwing their panties at you, your bar could use a reset."

Hmm. There was an interesting sort of fire in her eyes and he didn't quite know what to make of it. "Women? Where did that come from?"

"It seems I'm not the only one they're talking about in these parts. The word is spreading about the wealthy, good-looking man who is relocating to Blackwater Lake. And when the word gets out, and it will, that he's polite—" she fanned herself with her hand "—you will be in demand."

"Not if they know I'm married."

"You won't be for much longer," she reminded him.

It occurred to him that he would rather be in this nebulous state with her than single or married to anyone else. His next thought was that he needed a shrink to unravel the previous one. "I don't even know what to say to that."

"All I'm saying is watch your back. You've been warned."

"Got it."

"And don't be showing up the other guys by holding a woman's chair for her. You'll have no friends." She met his gaze. "Although I think you can probably count on family."

"Ellie is my half sister." Again, consulting a shrink crossed his mind.

"Do you only love her halfway?" Rose asked pointedly.

"Of course not." This conversation wasn't headed anywhere he wanted to go. "So, Miss Interior Designer. What do you think of this place?"

She glanced around, her expression assessing. "It's eclectic but that works. The gold, rust and green colors evoke the harvest theme and a subtext of a bountiful feast.

And there's a relaxed, country feel with the artistically placed items on the shelf. The hand pump, washboard, tin mugs and painted footstool are nice touches. It's cozy and comfortable."

"So, is that an endorsement? Or an article for *Better Homes and Gardens*?"

"It is two thumbs-up." She smiled, then said, "Now we need to check out the menu."

"Yeah." Although he would rather look at her. The way her eyes sparkled when she was needling him. And her face lit up when he made her laugh. She challenged his mind and teased his body just by being her.

A few minutes later a waitress came over to take their orders and the service was fast and flawless. He and Rose made small talk and shared a bottle of wine with the best bread and cranberry-walnut salad he'd had in a long time. The entrées—chicken marsala for him, trout almondine for her—would rival the best food he'd eaten in Los Angeles, New York, or Dallas. And then there was the dessert they decided to share.

"Oh, that's sinfully scrumptious." Rose chewed the first bite of the multilayered chocolate cake and closed her eyes in ecstasy.

Linc's body tightened at the expression on her face—she looked as if she was turned on and loving it. He badly wanted to be that man—the one who turned her on.

"So you like it?" He hoped his voice sounded normal to her because it sure didn't to him.

"*Like* is too ordinary a word for the way I feel about this cake."

He nearly groaned out loud when she took another bite and moaned, closing her eyes again. "Love then?"

"You're getting warmer."

That was for damn sure, but he hoped it didn't show.

There was a question in her eyes when she commented, "You're not eating any."

It would sound pretty dopey if he said he was feasting on the sight of her, just watching her pleasure. Not to mention a suggestive remark like that could violate the spirit of trust he was working for.

"I'm waiting to be a little less stuffed," he lied.

"If you wait too long there won't be any left." She took another bite to prove her point that she could eat it all.

He stuck his fork in, took a taste of melt-in-your-mouth goodness and understood her reaction. Almost better than sex. Those words, thank the Lord, did not come out of his mouth. All he said was, "Wow."

"I know, right?"

Maggie walked over to them, followed by the very attractive blonde he'd met at Bar None on ladies' night. "I see you're having the chocolate-cake experience."

"*Experience* is definitely the right word. This is the most delicious thing I have ever tasted in my life," Rose said.

"Then you can thank my friend, business partner and the chef here at the Harvest Café." She indicated the woman beside her. "Lucy Bishop, meet Rose Tucker and Lincoln Hart."

"Nice to meet you," Lucy said. "Linc and I have already met. I've heard a lot about you, Rose."

"From Aggie and Faith?" Linc asked wryly.

"Actually no," Maggie answered. "Your sister, Ellie."

Lucy looked from one to the other. "Rumor has it that you two are not quite divorced."

"Not exactly a rumor," Maggie clarified, "since Ellie flat-out told us."

"My sister is a lovely woman and many other wonderful things, but trustworthy with my personal life isn't one of them."

"Don't be mad at her," Lucy pleaded. "She shared it in a good way."

"It's hard to see exactly in what way that might be good." He looked at Rose and couldn't decide whether she was amused about this or bothered that their secret was out.

"We were talking about my upcoming wedding," Maggie said. "I'm engaged to Sloan Holden and we're planning it soon."

"I've met him. He's a good guy," Linc said.

"He is." Maggie glowed. "The conversation with Ellie turned to all the couples here in town who have recently taken the plunge into commitment."

Lucy held up her hand and ticked them off on her fingers. "There's Maggie, of course. Erin Riley and Jack Garner—"

"The best-selling writer?" There was a little awe in Rose's voice.

"Yes," Lucy confirmed. "And our own sheriff and the town photographer—Will Fletcher and April Kennedy."

"More and more people are calling it the Blackwater Lake effect." Lucy smiled at them as if that explained everything. "No one understands exactly how or why it happens, but relationship-challenged people come here and end up falling in love. Not me, of course, because I've sworn off men and already live here. But other people new to the area seem to fall under its spell."

"So when you say Ellie mentioned it in a good way," Rose said tentatively, "that means she is in favor of me and Linc—"

"Getting back together," Maggie said, finishing her thought. "Emotionally speaking, since you're still kind of married."

"Well, I hate to be a downer on that idea, but I'm only here to work." Rose shrugged.

"Don't write off the Blackwater Lake effect. This is where strange and unexplainable romantic things happen while you're 'working.'" Lucy made air quotes on the last word.

Rose shook her head. "At the risk of bursting the proverbial bubble, I'm not staying. Not relocating. Going back to Texas. There's nothing between Linc and me. He's welcome to cozy up to any and every woman in Montana. With my blessing."

"Famous last words." Maggie gave her friend a knowing look, then smiled at them. "I hope you enjoyed your dinner."

"Very much," Linc and Rose said together.

"Glad to hear it." Lucy nodded. "We look forward to seeing you in here often."

Linc had watched Rose's interaction with the other two women and wondered if she was protesting too much. It crossed his mind that her "nothing between us" comment could be a defensive reaction. There was that fire in her eyes again when she mentioned him in connection with all the women in Montana and the edge to her voice when she said it.

He had a suspicion that she was jealous and liked the thought of that very much.

Chapter Twelve

"You don't believe in the Blackwater Lake effect, do you?" Rose asked when they were in the car and headed back to Ellie's.

"Uh-oh." Linc's grin was visible in the vehicle's dashboard lights. "You're starting to trust and maybe falling a little in love with me. And judging by the tone of your voice, you're not happy about it."

"Oh, please…" Hopefully she'd put enough sarcasm in those two words to keep him from guessing how close he'd come to the truth. "I'm being serious."

"Me, too. Stranger things have happened. Think about it. Ellie came here for work and fell in love with Alex, then stayed." He glanced over for a moment. "Sound familiar?"

One beat passed, then two. Finally she said, "Tell me that you're not saying that I'm going to stay here in Blackwater Lake. With you."

"You have to admit you're attracted to me."

"No, I don't," she said emphatically. But just because she wouldn't admit there was some truth in his words didn't make them wrong.

"See there? You practically agreed with me."

"I did not." She huffed out a breath. "Those two ladies are very nice and the Harvest Café is a fabulous place. I want to try ice cream in the little store connected to it before I go back to Dallas—"

"But?"

"How did you know there's a *but*?"

"Because that's what you do."

"I have no idea what you mean." She stared at him. "What do I do?"

"Before you deliver the *but*, there's always a compliment, another nice comment, then—*bam*. Zinger."

"I do not." Then she laughed because that's exactly what she'd been about to do. "*But* Lucy and Maggie are romantics who own a business. For them talking up the Blackwater Lake effect could be a marketing tool. And part of a public relations campaign."

"Didn't Maggie's fiancé come to town for work? Then he fell in love and stayed."

"Speaking of romantics," she said pointedly, "when did you turn into one? Is there a full moon on Friday the thirteenth? Is it causing a ripple in the Blackwater Lake effect? When those two events intersect a confirmed bachelor turns into a romantic instead of a werewolf?"

"I'm not a bachelor," he reminded her. "I'm your husband."

"But you only recently became aware of that, which means for nearly ten years you've had a bachelor mindset," she argued. "A status you intend to maintain forever-after when the divorce is final."

"And what do you want after the divorce, Rose?"

"A traditional family. Something I never had. Something that looks a lot like what your sister has with Alex and Leah." His sudden switch from teasing to serious and sensitive threw her off balance, startled her. Otherwise she probably would have given him a flippant instead of honest answer.

"Then I'm sorry things didn't work out with Chandler." That didn't sound the least bit sincere. "I hope it wasn't my fault and another sin to add to my long list."

"No."

Again he glanced over briefly. "That doesn't sound very heartfelt."

"It was completely heartfelt." But no way was she going to say more. Otherwise she'd have to admit kissing him had gotten to her. So much so that she knew what she felt for Chandler would never be the kind of love that would be the foundation for what she so badly wanted. "And I'd rather not talk about him."

"You do realize that shutting down the Chandler topic just makes me want to know more."

"What are you? Twelve? You want what you can't have? Or you don't know the meaning of the word *no*?"

"Both." He grinned. "Not about the being twelve part."

"Not chronologically anyway." He was a man. The only one who had ever touched her heart and, she was afraid, the only man who ever would.

He turned right into his sister's driveway. "Looks like Ellie and Alex have a visitor."

Beside the truck and minivan Rose saw an unfamiliar luxury SUV. "I don't remember her saying anything about company coming."

"She didn't to me," he said.

He parked the car and got out, then came around and opened her door. Definitely he was raised with manners, she thought, sliding out. He put his hand to the small of her back as, side by side, they walked in the front door. The sound of voices became louder the closer they got to the kitchen.

Rose felt him tense and looked up. He was frowning. She'd seen him edgy and annoyed, but she'd never seen him look like that. "What's wrong?"

"That's not company." His voice was rough, harsh with emotion.

"How do you know?"

In the kitchen standing by the island was an older couple in their late fifties to early sixties. The woman was beautiful and had probably been stunning in her younger years. The man was distinguished and still handsome. Ellie and Alex were there, too, and everyone stopped talking when they saw Linc.

"Rose," he said, "this is Katherine and Hastings Hart, my mother and her husband." His voice was cold and bitter when he said, "You should have told me they were coming, Ellie."

"Why? So you could have disappeared?" she said. "Everyone is aware of your situation, Linc."

"Including all of Blackwater Lake by now. Because for some reason you felt it was your mission to make sure that the details of my life were available for public consumption."

"Not the public everyone," she said, defending herself. "I meant your family."

The older woman smiled tensely as she moved closer. "It's very nice to meet you, Rose. Hastings and I look forward to—"

"What?" Linc took a half step in front of Rose, almost a protective move. "Getting to know her? What's the point? Why are you really here?"

The older woman looked a little sad and uncertain, but unapologetic as she met his gaze. "We're here because we want to know what's going on. This rift, this silent treatment from you, has gone on long enough. You're married and never said a word to us?"

"You gave up the right to information about my life when you made the decision to lie to me."

"Lincoln—" Hastings Hart snapped out the name in a deep commanding voice. "You will treat your mother with the respect she deserves."

"That's the thing. Respect is earned and—"

"Linc—" Rose grabbed his hand. "Let's take a walk. Now." Before tugging him back the way they'd come in, she looked at the older couple. "Mrs. Hart, Mr. Hart, it's a pleasure to meet you both."

Sometimes retreat was the better part of valor and this was one of those times. She knew Ellie felt the same when she heard the other woman say behind them, "Mom, Dad, let him go."

At the front door she opened it and they walked outside into the cool night air, but the tension came with them. She expected Linc to pull his hand out of hers but he didn't. She could feel the anger and bitterness in the way he gripped her fingers so tightly.

"Why did you drag me out of there?" he demanded.

"First of all, I didn't drag you. You might be acting like a twelve-year-old, but you're too big for me to do that." She took a deep breath of the cool, fresh air. "Second, I thought it prudent to give you a time-out before you said anything else that you'll regret."

"Anything else implies that I regret what I just said. For the record, I don't. They had it coming. And more."

"Isn't it a beautiful view?"

Ellie and Alex's house was on a hill facing the lake.

Across the street there was grass, a sidewalk and railing. A full moon shone down, highlighting the water and mountains and a refreshing spring breeze cooled her hot cheeks.

"I love the ornate streetlights and the lovely benches along the path. Let's walk over there."

Without a word, Linc lifted her hand and settled it into the bend of his elbow, then escorted her across the street to the walkway as if he was accompanying her into an elegant ballroom. Just a short while ago he'd told her he was raised with manners and she'd just met the people responsible for raising him that way.

She wasn't a betrayal virgin but decided not to point out that he was the man who'd initiated her. Part of her understood why he'd left and wanted to hug him and make the bitterness go away. Or be angry at them in solidarity with him. But he'd been running for ten years and it was time to face this head-on.

"Don't you think it's a beautiful night?" she asked.

"It was until they showed up."

"They love you, Linc."

"They have a funny way of showing it."

"Not really." She knew he was going to push back on this. "Nothing says love more than coming all this way to support their son."

"I'm not—"

"Let me stop you right there. Tonight at the café you pulled out my chair and impressed the heck out of Maggie and Lucy. You told me you were raised with manners. Those were your words. You were brought up to be a gentleman—a good man. The woman and man in your sister's kitchen did that and you should thank them."

"For lying to me the whole time?" He sounded incredulous.

"You never knew. They treated all four of their children the same or you would have felt different and known something was up. You are the good and productive man you are because of the decision they made. Would you be what you are today if they'd told you from the time you could understand that you had a different father? Or maybe when you were a teenager?" She made a face. "That would have been ugly."

"They were just protecting themselves," he growled.

"No. They were protecting you."

"It doesn't matter," he said.

"It does. They always had your best interests at heart because they love you." She put her other hand on his arm, holding tight. "I never had one father. You're lucky enough to have two."

"No—"

"You do. One who raised you and one biological. Just because you're a stubborn ass and refuse to talk to either one doesn't make it not true."

He looked down at her for several long moments and his frown eased a fraction as he settled his big hand over both of hers. "You're brutally honest."

"I try." She smiled. "And here's a thought. Forgive them, Linc."

"Why should I?"

"Because they're human and everyone makes mistakes. But don't do it for them. Do it for you. Forgiveness is the only way to move on and find peace."

The moonlight revealed a glint in his eyes. "Are you willing to practice what you preach and forgive me? I'm human."

"No way," she teased.

"Way." He brushed his thumb over the back of her hand. "I made a big mistake when I left you and I regret it very much. Can you ever forgive me for it?"

"Yes. I already have. You were an idiot."

"Don't sugarcoat it. Tell me how you really feel," he said wryly.

"Brutally honest, remember? The mistake you made was in not talking to me about it. Now I can see a little of what you went through, so forgiveness isn't that hard. Don't you think your mother and father—he is your father," she said when he started to protest. "Don't make another mistake and walk away again without talking things over. Don't be an idiot."

The corners of his mouth turned up just a little. "Something tells me if I head in that direction you're going to have a little to say about it."

"Like I said, you're an honorable man. You'll do the right thing."

In some ways that was a bigger problem for her. She believed he *was* a good man and his betrayal had been an isolated incident, a decision made during a deeply personal and chaotic time in his life. She trusted him and now there was nothing standing in the way of her falling for him. That was bad because she believed he hadn't lied to her when he said that he would never marry again.

That meant falling for him was in direct conflict with having the traditional family she'd always dreamed of.

Linc couldn't sleep.

His mother and Hastings were occupying the downstairs guest room. As if that didn't ratchet up his tension enough, Rose was just a few steps away and he wanted her so badly it felt as if his head was going to explode.

The thought of having his hands on her, being able to kiss every square inch of her bare skin, was driving him crazy. When he managed to doze off, dreams of her yanked him out of it. But he wasn't just drawn to her curvy body.

If she hadn't been with him earlier, first to keep him from saying something he'd regret, then talking him off the ledge, it would have been a lot uglier.

The best way to say thanks for the support was to leave her alone. She wanted marriage and family, but he wasn't the guy who could give that to her.

"Damn it." He threw off the sheet and got up.

There was a really good single malt Scotch in the house and he knew where Alex kept it. Very quietly he tiptoed downstairs in his sweatpants and T-shirt. Light from the full moon trickled in through the high family room windows as he made his way to the kitchen.

He turned on the light over the stove so he could see and still not disturb anyone else in the house. As soundlessly as possible he retrieved the bottle from the "useless for much of anything but liquor" cupboard above the refrigerator but had no idea where to find an appropriate glass. He grabbed a coffee mug and splashed some Scotch into it, then started to put the cap back on the bottle.

"Leave it out." The familiar female voice came from behind him.

He turned to face her. There were shadows in the far corners of the room but he saw Katherine Hart on the other side of the island. "Mom."

"I'm glad you're up. I wasn't quite sure how I was going to reach that bottle. Would you pour me a glass?"

"Are you sure? It's the middle of the night."

"I can't sleep," she said. "It helps."

"Yeah. Me, too." He got out another mug and poured her what looked like an appropriate amount, then came around the island and handed it to her.

Side by side they sat on the high bar chairs at the island and stared into the dim kitchen while sipping the liquor.

Katherine finished first and wrapped her hands around the mug. "So, you and Rose are married?"

"Ellie told you all this."

"I'd like to hear it from you."

"Why?" he asked.

"I don't know." She stared into the empty cup, sad and deflated somehow. Very unlike the formidable woman she was. "I guess I've just missed talking to you. About books, movies, what's going on in the world. In your world."

If he was being honest, he would admit to feeling that void, too. "You have three other kids for that."

"I love all of my children." She glanced at him for a moment. "A mother isn't supposed to have favorites and I celebrate all the qualities that make each of you different and wonderful. But I will admit that you have a special place in my heart, Linc."

"Why?" He figured this was her kissing up to make amends for lying to him.

"You brought Hastings and me back together." She met his gaze directly, unashamed.

That surprised him. "I don't believe you. Your marriage was in shambles. Finding out you were pregnant must have made things worse."

"It was hard," she admitted. "But the way your father— and don't you dare say he's not—stepped up made me realize how much I love him. He took responsibility for neglecting me and his children, then promised nothing would take priority over family again. He could have told me he loves me from here to the moon but that would just have been words. He was there for me during the pregnancy and your birth. He held you, embraced you as his son and never in any way treated you differently from your brothers and sister." Her eyes were fierce with protective-ness for her husband. "He showed me then how much he loved me. Because of you. We both love you in a special way for bringing out the best in us, bringing us closer than we'd ever been."

Linc didn't know how to respond to that. So he said, "Ten years ago Rose and I fell madly in love. We wanted to be married and couldn't wait. So we went to Las Vegas."

"Why didn't you say something to us?"

"I didn't want you to judge, I guess. Be disappointed."

"What makes you think I would have been?" she asked.

"Rose was very young."

"So were you."

He shrugged. "And we just wanted to keep it between us for a little while."

"Then your biological father paid you a visit and the world as you knew it changed," she said. "And you ended the marriage."

"I thought so." He sipped some Scotch and wasn't sure if that was the only reason for the fire in his belly. Somehow telling all this to his mother brought everything back as if it happened yesterday. That feeling of being ripped in half when he faced Rose knowing he was a fraud. "I don't know who I am."

"You're my son." It was the mom voice, the one that did not allow for argument.

"That only gives me half the answers. I'm not a legitimate Hart."

"Have you seen your biological father?"

"Just that one time," he said.

Shadows highlighted the absolute and utter regret on her gently lined face. "It was wrong of me to lie to you, son. I won't offer excuses, but you can believe the decision was made with your best interests being the only priority."

He thought about Rose's comment that there was no good time to tell him. But he wasn't quite ready to relinquish the resentment that had supported him all this time. "You could have shared custody with him."

"That was an option," she agreed. "But there were two things that stopped me. Number one, visitations with him would have set you apart from your siblings and made you feel separate from the family."

He could see how that might happen. Not being a part of the Hart domestic unit had never crossed his mind growing up. He'd been secure and happy, had an idyllic childhood. And it wouldn't have been. But still… "And what was the second thing?"

"Your biological father's career. To claim a child that was conceived not only out of wedlock, but with a woman separated from her husband and a client, as well, could have destroyed his reputation. He was willing and relieved to bow out of the picture."

"So you thought I would never find out unless I needed a kidney and none of the Harts were a match?"

"Yes. Then he changed the rules." The bitterness in her voice rivaled his own.

It crossed his mind that was possibly a trait he'd inherited from her. "Why did he tell me?"

"You'll have to ask him that question."

The familiar anger swelled inside him. "And what if I don't want to see him?"

"That's your choice, of course, but there are things only he can tell you," Katherine said gently. "He can fill in the blanks. I know I've lost your trust and along with it the right to offer advice. So I'll just say this. You're caught between two worlds and that's holding you back." Hesitantly she put her hand on his arm.

It didn't escape his notice that he was no longer prepared and guarded, ready to withdraw from her touch. "I'm fine."

"You'll hate me for saying this, but I'm your mother

and you're the opposite of fine." Apparently the maternal contact made her bolder. More like the mother lion he remembered she'd always been. "Since you left Rose, there's been no one you cared about."

"How do you know that?"

"If you'd wanted to get married again, you would have known there was no divorce from her."

"Fair enough."

"I want you to be happy and you're not," she said. "I don't know what's holding you back but I have a suggestion where to start looking. Talk to your biological father. You don't need anyone's permission, especially mine, so take this advice for what it's worth. Don't think about sparing me or being disloyal to your family. Do it for yourself. And keep in mind that there's room for everyone in your life."

"That's what Rose said," he murmured. Actually she'd told him that she never knew her father and he was lucky to have two who cared about him.

For the first time his mother smiled. "Obviously she and I agree on something, so I have to say she's a bright girl. You were a little bit of an idiot to walk away from her."

"That seems to be the majority opinion. In my defense, it has to be said that hindsight is twenty-twenty." But he'd left her *because* he loved her so damn much. His concern had been for her, sparing her the long, slow painful death of love because he was an imposter. Never mind that he hadn't known. "I did what I felt was right."

"I know. But—"

"What?" he asked.

"Never mind." Katherine slid off the bar chair. "Probably I shouldn't stick my nose into your business."

"Why stop now?" The corners of his mouth turned up.

"Don't be fresh," she teased.

"Seriously," he said. "I'd really like to know what you were going to say."

"Okay." She sighed. "Granted I didn't see you and Rose together for very long this evening, but I got the impression that she was protective of you. Call me silly, but there was a spark. Maybe I'm just a romantic."

Maybe a romantic streak was something else he'd inherited from his mother. On the way home from dinner Rose had accused him of having one. It sure hadn't felt that way for the last ten years. But since seeing her again…

"It's really late," Katherine said after glancing at the digital time display on the microwave. "Oh, I almost forgot, what with all the commotion earlier. Ellie signed for a certified packet that came for you and Rose. It's on the desk in the office. I wasn't prying but the return address indicates it's from a law firm."

The divorce papers had arrived. "Thanks for letting me know."

"You're welcome. I need to get some sleep and so do you."

Easy for her to say, he thought. She would climb into bed next to her husband. But he…

Had a woman upstairs who wouldn't be his wife for very much longer. And he still wanted her as badly as he had ten years ago. He'd promised himself that she was going to trust him before this was all over. And the divorce papers in the study were here to end it. That should have made him feel better.

It didn't.

Chapter Thirteen

Rose looked at the clock on the bedside table and groaned. It was the middle of the night and she hadn't slept much. And she wasn't the only one. A sliver of light coming from around the bathroom door indicated Linc was awake, too. It didn't take a genius to figure out that he was restless because of the earlier scene in the kitchen with his parents. That was a side of him he'd never showed her and she couldn't get it off her mind.

When they were together, he was always confident and a little cocky. Ten years ago his proposal had given her pause because she wondered whether or not she would be his equal in the relationship. She'd needed him desperately but wasn't sure he needed her. Then they got married and shortly afterward he'd left and her question was answered.

Or so she'd thought.

Now she knew he was going through a family crisis and chose to deal with it on his own. Earlier she'd walked him away from the ugly scene, then talked him through the resulting feelings. She was glad to do it but the emotion was bittersweet. If only he hadn't underestimated her when they were together, she could have helped him then and how different their lives would have been. They'd missed out on so much.

If only he hadn't shut her out. If only spending time with him hadn't rekindled her attraction. If only he hadn't sworn off commitment.

If only Linc would turn out the bathroom light. She looked at the clock again and frowned. For a man who set speed records for being camera-ready, he'd been in there a long time. Maybe he wasn't as okay after their talk as he'd led her to believe.

After a brief argument with herself, she decided to check on him. If she was wrong, it wouldn't be the first time there'd been bathroom awkwardness.

She threw back the covers and grabbed her robe from the foot of the bed, then slipped her arms into it. Barefoot, she walked to the door that was just barely open.

Knocking softly she said, "Linc?"

"I'm finished. It's all yours."

Something in his voice set off warning signals that he was troubled. "Are you all right?"

"Yes."

"Are you naked?"

"Why?"

"Because I'm coming in. Ready or not." She put her palm to the door and pushed it open wide. He was standing by the sink naked—except for the towel knotted at his waist.

"I'm sorry I woke you." He glanced at her and his mouth tightened before he looked away.

"Don't be sorry. I was already awake." She shrugged. "Couldn't sleep."

"Seems to be a lot of that going around at casa Mc-Knight."

His face was drawn, tired and tense. And completely vulnerable and sexy. An intoxicating combination. A light dusting of hair covered his broad chest and her palms tingled with the need to touch him. His hair was wet and he brushed it back from his forehead with both hands. The movement had the muscles in his arms rippling in a way that made her heart race.

Then her brain kicked back into gear and decrypted his words. "Who else can't sleep?"

"Besides me?"

"That's kind of what you implied." There was something he didn't want to talk about. "Who was up?"

"My mom. We just had a Scotch together in the kitchen."

"Well. I'm guessing you didn't tell her she gave up the right to have a drink with you because of the lie."

"No." One corner of his mouth quirked up.

She waited for him to say more and when he didn't she couldn't hold back the questions. "Did you talk? Did she talk? Or was there only silence?"

"There was talk," he offered.

"From who? You? Her?" Rose was getting frustrated at having to drag the information out of him.

"She apologized for lying. Said they made the decision so my life would be normal. And never expected bio-dad to change his mind and rat her out."

"You know, Linc, it occurs to me that you could debate the pros and cons of their decision and make an excellent case for the choice they made and the one they didn't. But here's the thing. They made the one they did and you grew up to be the exceptional man you are. There's no going back now."

"Is that your way of telling me to just get over it without actually saying the words?" One dark eyebrow went up questioningly.

"I suppose so. You're going to point out that it's easy for me to say and you'd be right. But what's the alternative?" She was being practical, not cavalier.

"I could continue to be hostile toward her."

"That's really mature," she said.

"As you have pointed out more than once I'm pretty good at juvenile behavior." His mouth twitched.

"Sooner or later we all have to grow up. Even you. Maybe it's time to cut her some slack."

"Maybe."

His voice was wistful and she saw the conflict darkening his eyes. That's the only reason she moved closer and put her hand on his arm—to convey her empathy and compassion. She'd expected his skin to be warm after his shower and was surprised that it wasn't. "Are you okay? Why are you cold?"

"Because I took a cold shower." His eyes darkened. "And no, I'm not anywhere near okay. Pretty much in the neighborhood of everything is screwed up."

"What is it? Are you sick?"

"No." He pulled his arm away almost angrily but the irritation was directed at himself. "Go back to bed. I'm sorry I bothered you."

He hadn't, not the way he meant. But she was bothered now. She closed the gap he'd opened between them and put her hand on his arm again. "Linc, why did you take a cold shower?"

"Why does a man ever do that?"

"Please answer my question," she said.

"Don't push it, Rose." He closed his eyes. "You know why and this isn't what you want."

"How do you know what I want?"

"Because I know you." He looked at her then and his gaze was full of frustration and anger and need. "You're sweet and honest. And you don't trust me."

"What if I've changed my mind? What if I do trust you?" She slid her fingers up to his shoulder and heard his quick intake of breath.

"I'm glad." He gripped her upper arms gently and set her away from him. "Believe me, this is the hardest thing I've ever done. I'm a jerk and an idiot, with public opinion swinging toward jackass, too. But I won't be the son of a bitch who's responsible for you hating yourself in the morning."

"I won't, Linc. Tell me you haven't felt what's going on between us."

"Of course I have." His low voice didn't take the edge off the explosive emotion. "But I won't take advantage of you."

"I want this. How is that you taking advantage?"

"Because you want vows and the whole nine yards and I can't make any promises."

Right this second she didn't give two hoots about anything but the knot of need in her belly that only he could relieve. She moved closer and he retreated, literally putting his back against the wall.

"I'm not going to argue with you," she said.

There was stubborn determination in his expression but the effort showed it was ragged around the edges. "Good, because I've made up my mind."

"Well, then this probably won't faze you at all."

She reached between them and released his towel, then felt it fall at her feet. After pressing herself against him, she stood on tiptoe, put her hands on his cheeks and pulled his face down to hers. Their lips came together in a gentle touch that belied the power of the chemistry boiling between them. For just a second she tasted his hesitation.

Then he said, "Damn it."

The words seemed to get rid of all his hang-ups because he wrapped his arms around her and kissed her like she'd never been kissed before. It was filled with ten years' worth of longing and deprivation and the friction of their mouths cranked up the heat, sent it coursing through her.

He slid his fingers into her hair, cupping the back of her head to make the contact more sure. The kiss went on forever and the room was filled with the harsh sound of their breathing. Suddenly he pulled back and looked at her, his gaze full of hunger and yearning just before he scooped her into his arms. This was happening and stopping it now was like trying to slow a locomotive with a spiderweb. Even if she wanted to, she couldn't do that.

"Your place or mine?" he asked, his voice rough with passion.

"Surprise me."

"Mine has condoms." He shrugged. "They're always in my travel bag. Are you judging?"

"Maybe after I'm finished being grateful." She wrapped her arms around his neck, then leaned in and kissed him just behind his ear.

"You're killing me," he groaned.

"Do you want me to stop?" She licked the spot she'd kissed, then blew on it.

"No." He shivered before his body tensed again.

He carried her into his room and set her in the middle of the bed. Her nightgown and robe were gathered up around her waist and he sat beside her, sliding his hand over her knee and higher to her thigh, before he gripped the hem and pulled both of them off in one smooth move.

Linc opened the nightstand drawer and rummaged around for something. With a triumphant grunt he removed a square packet and set it on the nightstand. Then he took her in his arms and together they slowly lowered to the mattress. A hard-charging heat surged through her when he kissed her neck, breasts, belly and hip.

Oh, God, he was killing her, but what a way to go. Her heart was pounding and she could hardly breathe. More important, she had to get closer. She pressed her body to his, arching her hips against him, showing him what she wanted and that waiting wasn't an option.

"I know, baby," he murmured against her neck.

In the next instant he opened the condom and put it on. Then he pressed her body into the mattress with his own and settled himself between her legs.

She held her breath as he prepared to enter her and sighed in satisfaction when he did. He moved inside her and the tension in her belly tightened deliciously with each thrust. Before she was ready, the bubble burst and pleasure rocked through her in wave after unbelievably powerful wave. He held her, kissed her and whispered tender words to her until the tremors subsided.

Then he settled his weight on his forearms and began to move again. She wrapped her legs around his waist and met him thrust for thrust until he buried his face in her neck and groaned as he found his own release.

Slowly their breathing returned to normal and he lifted his head to smile down at her. "I'll be right back. You don't have to go."

"Okay."

Her eyes closed but she felt the mattress dip as he left the bed and went into the bathroom. After a few moments the light went off and he slid in beside her again, pulling her close.

"You're just full of surprises, Rose."

Probably it was fatigue that made her say what she did next. She was tired and satisfied and happier than she could ever remember being. There were no reserves left to hold anything back and she didn't.

"I love you, Linc. I don't think I ever stopped." She felt his body tense and hurried to reassure him. "It's all right. I know you don't want to hear it but I needed to say the words. Don't worry. I don't expect anything. I just wanted to thank you for this."

"No." Tenderly he kissed her temple. "Thank you."

Barely awake now, she smiled and relaxed against his warmth, looking forward to waking up beside him.

Sometime during the night Rose went back to her own room, quietly shutting the two doors between them. As badly as she'd wanted to stay snuggled in Linc's arms, it was the discreet thing to do. Technically they were married but separated and if anyone happened to walk in and find them in bed together it would be awkward. Possibly requiring a clarification about what was going on and that was difficult since she didn't quite understand it herself.

Not the sex part. That was as easy as it was amazing. But the emotional consequences were much more complicated.

Oddly enough she'd gone back to sleep, but she was awake now and threw back the covers, stretching before rolling out of her own bed. In the bathroom she stared at the closed door to Linc's room and sighed. She was in love with him and he seemed to return the feeling, although he hadn't said so.

After turning on the water in the shower to warm it up,

she smiled at the door that separated them and realized
she hadn't been this happy in, well…ten years. Should she
invite him into the shower with her? Probably it would be
best not to disturb him. He needed sleep since they'd been
up pretty late. But she couldn't help hoping he would join
her and when it didn't happen she was a little disappointed.
Still she looked forward to seeing him.

Not so much his sister and parents.

Would she look any different to them? What if they
could tell she and Linc had had sex just by the expressions
on their faces or the way they acted around each other? Intimacy as powerful as what she'd shared with him changed
everything and there was no going back. She needed to
talk to him before facing his family.

She showered, dressed, did hair and makeup, giving
him as much time as possible to sleep before softly knocking on his door.

"Linc?" She listened for a response and didn't hear
anything. He was a sound sleeper so she knocked a little
louder. "Linc? Are you awake?"

It was time for him to be up anyway and she needed
coffee, so she opened the door, determined to move this
along faster. "Ready or not…"

His room was empty and the bed neatly made.

"Hmm," she said to herself. "It would seem that he let
me sleep in."

Plan B, she thought. There wouldn't be time to coordinate a plan before facing his family so she was going to
have to wing it. At least until she could get him alone to
talk about last night.

She'd told him she loved him and had never stopped. It
was clear now that without him she'd moved on but hadn't
really had a life. Being with him was the most important
thing and she was pretty sure he felt the same way about

her. He'd actually tried to talk her out of sleeping together in order to protect her. How could you not trust a man like that? How could she not love him? The rest would work itself out in time and now they had it.

Rose took one last look in the mirror, giving her tailored jeans, white blouse and loosely crocheted navy sweater the nod of approval. This look was casual enough for Blackwater Lake, but still professional.

"Coffee, here I come," she said to her reflection and hoped Linc would approve of the outfit.

But Linc wasn't in the kitchen. She saw Ellie and his mother sitting at the table with mugs of coffee in front of them. No sign of Mr. Hart or Linc.

Leah ran over and held out her arms. "Up!"

Rose smiled, more than happy to obey the order. "Good morning, Miss Leah. And did you have a good sleep last night?"

"Yes!" Did all children speak in exclamation points? Leah pointed to the two women. "Mama, Gammy. Look! Wo'!"

"She's been waiting for you." Ellie smiled fondly. "And how did you sleep last night?"

"Fine." Was her voice normal? Or did it sound like the voice of a woman who'd had sex with this woman's brother? Should she say more about how comfortable the bed was or just leave it there?

And where in the world was Linc?

She didn't trust herself to say his name without blushing a dozen shades of pink so didn't bring him up. "Good morning, Mrs. Hart."

"Same to you, Rose. But please call me Katherine."

"I will. Thanks."

"I'll pour you some coffee," Ellie said, standing. "And

you can put my spoiled-rotten child down anytime you want."

Rose hugged the sturdy little body close for a moment. "I like holding her."

"She gets heavy."

Katherine smiled as she looked at her granddaughter. "I can't believe how much she's grown since your dad and I last saw her."

"She's a cutie pie." Rose could practically feel her maternal instincts stirring and stretching as she studied the angelic face so close to hers. It wasn't the first time but this was definitely more powerful than ever before.

Was it sleeping with Linc that made her hormones stand up and shout "look at me"? Or just being around this precious little girl who was his niece? A little girl who was now squirming to get down. Rose set her on her feet, holding on until she was steady, and then Leah took off running into the adjacent family room.

"And now she's so over me," Rose said, laughing.

"A child's short attention span is both a blessing and curse." There was a regretful tone in Katherine's voice. "And when they grow up, you wish it was possible to distract them. Make them forget what's painful for them."

"I imagine so." Rose sat at the kitchen table where Ellie had set her mug, an invitation to join the conversation.

"I apologize that you had to see our scene last night, Rose. It wasn't pretty, but I thank you for being there for my son."

"Of course." And she knew that mother and son had talked, but wasn't sure they'd buried the hatchet. As far as attention spans were concerned, hers had been pretty thoroughly drawn in by the sight of his bare chest and muscular arms. Not to mention that he was wearing nothing but a towel, which was so easily removed—

The older woman was taking her measure, something any loving and concerned mother would do. "So you and Linc are married."

"Just a little bit." Rose could feel the dozen shades of pink starting in her cheeks and took a sip of her coffee. Let them chalk the blush up to a hot flash of caffeine. "It's pretty complicated."

"Yes. It would seem so." Katherine nodded. "But I think you still care about each other—"

"Mom, don't pry," Ellie warned. "You know he hates it when you do that."

"Yes. But since he's giving me the cold shoulder I don't have much to lose with Linc, do I?" The older woman sighed wearily.

"He'll come around," Ellie said sympathetically.

"I'm not so sure. It's been ten years," her mother pointed out.

"But you two are finally talking. And drinking together," Ellie said. She looked at Rose. "They couldn't sleep last night and ended up having a Scotch together."

"Ah." Rose was careful not to let on that she already knew about that.

"I'd hoped it was progress," his mother admitted. "But what am I to think with him leaving so suddenly. Obviously I said something wrong."

Rose had the coffee mug halfway to her lips and froze at the words. Linc was gone? Her whole body went cold.

"I already told you—" Ellie patted her mother's hand reassuringly "—his note said he had to go to Dallas."

Why? Rose wanted to ask because he hadn't told her he was going but managed to keep from saying anything.

"And why would he do that?" Katherine asked instead. "Except to get away from me."

Or me, Rose thought. Because she'd said she loved him.

"He still has business in Dallas and probably had something that needed his personal attention," Ellie pointed out. "He probably told Rose where he was going and why."

They both looked at her for an explanation and she wanted the earth to open up and swallow her whole. What in the world was she going to say? That she was the reason he couldn't get out of here fast enough?

She pulled herself together and said, "He mentioned something about details he needed to take care of."

"See?" Ellie looked triumphantly at her mother. "Not everything is about you."

Rose managed to choke down some of the breakfast Ellie made for her. She was even able to converse a little bit, laugh in all the right places, in spite of the buzzing in her head.

Linc left without a word after she slept with him.

Finally the ordeal of keeping up appearances was over and Ellie wouldn't hear of her helping to clean up the kitchen. She and her mother would handle it, then they were off for a day at the mall.

"You should come shopping with us," Ellie suggested.

"If only." Rose forced a smile. "I really need to work."

"My brother is a slave driver."

"He is many things," Rose said diplomatically. "Have fun, you two."

She escaped down the hall to her temporary office and closed the door behind her. And that's when she got the final blow. On the desk was a big official-looking packet from Mason Archer. It had been opened so Linc obviously knew what was inside.

Their divorce papers.

A feeling of déjà vu crushed her heart. The marriage was over and this time he hadn't even had the guts to face her before he left. If only she could fault him for taking advantage of her but he'd told her straight out he didn't want commitment and she hadn't asked for one. He even tried to talk her out of sleeping with him, but she'd pushed.

And now he was gone. At least he'd kept his word and stayed around until the divorce papers came. Then he'd reverted to his default behavior and disappeared without an explanation.

She couldn't continue this job and it was going to cost her everything—her business and her heart. And she had no one to blame but herself.

Chapter Fourteen

Linc decided to take his mother's advice and get some questions answered. He'd left Rose sleeping because after she said she'd never stopped loving him he had no fricking idea what to say to her. After taking the private jet back to Dallas, now he was going to talk to the only person who could give him the answers he was looking for.

It was nearing traditional quitting time when he walked into the offices of Pierce and Associates, Attorneys at Law, LLC. The lobby was a combination of rich, dark wood, glass, mirrors and plants. Tasteful elegance that signified wealth and prosperity.

He stopped at a desk where a young man was typing at a computer. The nameplate read Brandon Riggs. He wore a dark suit and blue silk tie, and had his brown hair slicked back off his forehead.

Brandon looked up from the monitor. "May I help you?"

"I'd like to see Robert Pierce."

"Do you have an appointment?"

"No. But I'm pretty sure he'll see me. Would you let him know that Lincoln Hart is here?"

The young man's eyebrows went up as he grabbed the phone and relayed the message. He listened for a few moments, then met Linc's gaze and finally said, "Okay, I'll send him right up."

"Thanks," Linc said.

"His office is on the top floor."

"I know." And not because that's where Linc's would be. The need to do that might be a hereditary thing, but he knew where the office was by gathering all the information available on this guy. Although that was all just facts. None of the data could tell him whether or not he had the DNA of a son of a bitch.

Linc took the elevator to the tenth floor and it opened to a thickly carpeted reception area with a desk in the center. A middle-aged woman was standing behind it.

"Mr. Pierce said to go right in, Mr. Hart. May I get you something? Coffee? Sparkling water? Scotch?"

"No, thanks." He'd had more than enough coffee and another cup might just make his head explode. And a drink? Not a good idea.

"All right then. I'll say good night." She slid the strap of her purse over her shoulder. "Have a good evening."

"You, too." He'd have an evening but whether or not it was good remained to be seen.

There were double, dark-wood doors straight ahead and an ornate nameplate proclaiming, in large letters, Robert Pierce.

"Here goes nothing."

He walked over and took a deep breath before knocking once and opening the door. The man who had loomed large in his mind for ten years sat behind a big desk covered with files and papers. His tie was loosened and the sleeves of his white dress shirt were rolled to midforearm. Linc studied him for several moments—the strong chin, brown hair liberally shot with silver, blue eyes—looking for a resemblance to himself. He wasn't very good at seeing that sort of thing, but wondered if he had any feature that was unmistakably from Robert Pierce.

The man stood and came around the desk, stopping several feet from him. "Hello, Linc. I'm glad you came to see me."

"I didn't do it for you."

"You look like your mother."

"Maybe that's why no one ever questioned my paternity all those years I thought I was a Hart. I never once suspected I had a bio-dad."

"You make me sound like a science experiment."

"Welcome to my world," Linc growled.

The man looked down for a moment, then met his gaze. "You're pissed off about being deceived."

"Hell, yes. Wouldn't you be?" It was so much deeper than anger. "Can you blame me?"

"And you want to know why I broke my word and approached you."

"Yeah, I do. Because you look pretty healthy to me and unless you needed a kidney or bone-marrow transplant from your only living relative, there's no good reason for doing that to me."

"You're right." He held out his arms, showing he was trim, fit all these years later. "I'm a selfish bastard. That's all I've got."

"Are you serious?" The admission enraged Linc. "You turned my life upside down and cost me my wife. And it was all about you? I have the DNA of a selfish, self-absorbed ass?"

"Not just mine. There's hope for you because your mother is in there, too." No anger surfaced in the man's voice, just sadness and the absence of hope.

That made Linc wonder. "Did you make it a habit to sleep with clients who were separated from their husbands?"

"I don't expect you to believe this." His mouth pulled tight for a moment. "But I never did that before her and I haven't done it since."

"Really? Why should I accept that as true?"

"Because I've never met another woman before or since like Katherine."

There was such abject misery and longing in the man's face that Linc figured either he was a very good actor or it was the truth. If he was right about the latter, he felt sorry for this guy. "You're in love with her?"

"Yes."

"But that was thirty-four years ago. You weren't even together that long."

Robert put his hands in the pockets of his slacks. "Do you believe in love at first sight?"

An image of Rose popped into his mind. She was walking toward him down a hallway at Hart Industries and smiled at him for the first time. He felt as if she'd just ripped his heart out of his chest, in the best way possible. From that moment, Linc had been determined to make her his.

"Yes," he finally said.

"Then you know how it feels to put someone else's happiness before your own."

"I do." It's why he'd walked away from Rose, to keep the ugliness of his life from infecting hers.

"Katherine told me she was pregnant and for just a few moments I was on top of the world. Then she said her husband knew about the baby and me. In spite of what she'd done they were reconciling. She said they were willing to work out a visitation agreement if I wanted."

"So it was your idea to pretend I didn't exist?" His mother hadn't lied.

"Yes." There was regret in his blue eyes. "I'd just joined the firm. As you might imagine it's frowned on for an attorney to take advantage of a client and sleep with her."

Linc winced. He'd had the taking-advantage conversation with Rose before sleeping with her. Then she kissed him and he just had nothing left to fight the wanting her. Hurting her was the last thing he'd ever intended but when sanity returned, so had the guilt.

"You bowed out," Linc said.

Robert nodded. "I promised her I would never see you or make a claim on you. Because I knew it would be easier on her that way."

That was a new perspective.

"That doesn't bode well for my positive DNA profile since we both know you didn't keep that promise." Linc dragged his fingers through his hair. "If I inherited your traits, I can expect to be a lying weasel and an egocentric bastard."

The other man didn't even blink. "That's one way of looking at it."

"How would you suggest I look at what you just told me?"

"Let me frame this for you—"

Anger rolled through Linc at the man's absolute composure. "Don't lawyer your way out of this."

"Hard not to when my career is all I have. I've been married four times and number four is about to implode. I'm alone and have no one to carry on my name."

"So you have commitment problems." This was exactly the reason Linc refused to let anyone in.

"It's not about commitment. I kept looking for a woman to be the love of my life. The problem was I'd already met her and there was no way to replace that since she's one of a kind." He sighed. "I never had a chance with her because she left Hastings but didn't stop loving him."

"How did he reconcile what she did?" Linc wondered.

"You'd have to ask him."

Suddenly Linc's anger evaporated and he felt nothing but sorry for this man. "I guess it's safe to say I didn't inherit your way with words because I have no idea what to say to that."

"There isn't anything to say." Robert rested a hip on the corner of his desk. "I, on the other hand, need to apologize for blowing up your life the way I did. I really am sorry and there's no defense for my actions."

Linc knew what loneliness felt like and was magnanimous enough to admit it could make any man a little crazy. "I believe you and accept your apology."

"If I can make it up to you… If there's anything I can do, just let me know."

The man was a divorce lawyer, but the paperwork was already done. He remembered the packet he'd left on the desk at Ellie's. He'd never forget the lonely, empty feeling that rolled through him when he saw them. "My divorce is already taken care of."

Robert looked puzzled. "Did you get married again?"

"No. Same woman." He explained what happened and found himself telling this man about hiring Rose to decorate his condo.

"So, you're still married to the woman you fell in love with at first sight?"

"Yes."

"Do you still love her?" Robert met his gaze for several moments. "Look, I know I'm the last person you'd ever want to confide in, but I have to say this. Just chalk it up to the voice of experience."

"What?"

"If you're lucky enough to find love, don't walk away from it."

Linc nodded, feeling lighter somehow, as if the rock sitting on his chest had just been lifted. Animosity went poof, too. Robert Pierce wasn't a bad guy, just a tragic one. He fell in love and it hadn't worked out for him.

"Thanks for seeing me," he said.

"Anytime." Robert shook the hand he held out. "My door is always open if you need anything. A kidney or bone-marrow transplant."

"That might explain where my smart-ass streak comes from." Linc smiled sheepishly. "Should I apologize?"

"Not on my account."

"Okay, then. I'll get out of here and let you get back to it."

A feeling of peace settled over him as he left the office and took the elevator to the first floor. His biological father wasn't anything like what he'd been picturing all this time. He seemed a decent, honest man—one he would like to know better. Rose was right. There was room in his life for two dads. Just as he stepped onto the street the cell phone in his pocket vibrated. He checked the caller ID and saw that it was Ellie. Again. He'd been dodging her calls and no longer felt the need to do that.

He hit talk. "Hey, sis. I have something to tell you—"

"Me first." That was her mom voice and put the fear of God into anyone who heard it. "You did it again, moron. Are you really that clueless? Or did you deliberately shoot yourself in the foot?"

"What are you talking about?"

"The lone wolf lives." There was a mother lode, no pun intended, of angry sarcasm in her voice. "You get divorce papers, then walk out on Rose without a word. Again. What the heck is wrong with you?"

The meaning of what she said hit him like a brick to the head. Apparently along with the smart-ass gene he'd inherited the selfish one from bio-dad. He'd only been thinking about what he needed. Oh, God… "I have to talk to her."

"Good luck with that. I don't think there's anything you can say that she wants to hear. For the record? That goes for me, too."

"Ellie, wait—" There was a click and he knew she'd just hung up on him.

Crap and double crap. Apparently he was in the lead for the "jackass of the year" award.

"I can't believe he walked out like that." Rose was back in Texas and a whole week had gone by since Linc left without a word.

Her friend Vicki had come over to her apartment for a trash-talking marathon. She'd been in the kitchen pouring two glasses of wine and set one down in front of Rose. "I'm sorry, honey. It was a no-win situation. Damned if you do, damned if you don't."

"Now I'm double damned." Because he broke her heart again. She added, "I quit his stinkin' job."

"You know you signed a contract." Her friend was also her lawyer.

"He can just sue me." She scooted forward on the couch and took her long-stemmed glass, then sipped some wine. "You can't get blood from a turnip. I'm not even worth his trouble."

"If he gets mad enough you might be." Vicki was sitting at the other end of the couch. "Have you heard from him?"

"He's called every day. Multiple times."

"So you've talked to him."

Rose shook her head. "I don't pick up."

"See, that's where the 'not ticking him off' part comes in. He's really holding all the cards."

Not to mention the grip he had on her heart, Rose thought. She knew how this process was going to go, having been through it with Linc once before. Right now anger sustained her. She was mad as hell and calling him every nasty name she knew helped to stoke her fury. But sooner or later it would subside because maintaining this elevated level of resentment took an awful lot of energy.

When it faded, the pain would come rushing in and threaten to overwhelm her. This time it just might and she'd never recover. The satisfaction of getting over him before had kept her going. Now she knew getting over him was nothing more than a pipe dream.

"He's a pig." Rose refused to give up her "stoking the anger" strategy. "Only a pig would throw around his weight like that and hassle a penniless, hardworking interior designer who's just trying to earn an honest living."

"He really hurt you, didn't he?" Vicki's brown eyes brimmed with sympathy.

"I won't let that be true."

"You slept with him." It wasn't a question.

Rose had not revealed that information to her friend. "You don't know that."

"Yeah, I do. You wouldn't have had sex with him if you didn't love him." Vicki shrugged. "This is me. I know you."

She didn't want to talk about that. "His family is incredibly down-to-earth and nice. I met his parents, his brother and his sister, Ellie. You'd like her, Vee. The three of us could have been really good friends if her brother wasn't such a... I've officially run out of words bad enough to call him."

"Just as I thought. You're in love with him."

"Stop saying that. What difference does it make anyway?"

"Well..." Vicki thought for a moment. "There could be a reason he left suddenly. A situation you are not aware of. Mitigating circumstances."

"You're such a lawyer." Rose drained the wine in her glass. "He left without a word to anyone. Not even his sister. If possible, I think she's more upset with him than I am."

"Still, maybe you should hear his side of the story."

"Again with the lawyer point of view," Rose said. "This isn't a court of law and I don't have to listen to anything he has to say. One time walking out and disappearing for a couple of years is something maybe you could shrug off. But twice is a pattern. Fool me once, shame on you. Fool me twice, shame on me. If I listen to anything he has to say now, it makes me too stupid to live."

Vicki sighed. "I get where you're coming from. But, and this is me being your lawyer, you might want to have a conversation with the man. In my experience, not talking is a good way to get sued. Lack of conversation ratchets up tension and animosity. It doesn't have to be personal. Smooth over the breach of contract."

"As much as I hate to admit it, you make a good point." Rose saluted the other woman with her empty wineglass even as every part of her rejected the idea of discussing anything with Lincoln Hart.

"So, return his call. While I'm here to legally advise you."

Rose both craved and dreaded hearing Linc's voice. It

was bad enough listening to the voice-mail messages. The sound of his words in deep, husky tones broke her heart a little more every time. She would rather bury her head in the sand and leave her backside exposed.

She wanted to push back against the legal advice. The problem was Vicki *did* have a point. Rose had terminated her contract without fulfilling her legal obligation. Her signature was on the paper and he had the money to make her life miserable. Legally speaking, since she was already miserable in a very personal way.

"I'll consider it," Rose said. "But in the spirit of full disclosure I should probably tell you that I've already ignored your advice once."

"I know," Vicki said drily. "You took the job."

"Thanks for not saying 'I told you so.'" Rose knew her friend was trying to look sympathetic instead of smug and the effort was much appreciated. "Considering that I did it anyway, I guess you could say that I've not listened to you twice."

"Oh, dear Lord, what else did you do?"

"I signed the divorce papers."

"Please tell me the terms are generous to you," the other woman begged.

"I could do that," she said, "if I'd actually read them."

"Oh, pickles." Her friend groaned. "Kids. They don't call. They don't write. They don't pay attention to excellent professional advice."

"You have to understand. I found them right after he walked out. I was…feeling a lot of emotions. You could probably say my signature was knee-jerk."

Vicki slapped a hand to her forehead. "What am I going to do with you?"

Rose didn't get a chance to respond to the question because her cell phone rang. She picked it up and looked at the caller ID. "It's Linc."

"Answer it."

"I don't want to."

"You wanted to know what you can do for me. That would be to talk to him." It rang again. "Now."

Rose stared at the other woman for several moments, then sighed and hit the talk button. "This is Rose Tucker."

There was a brief hesitation on the other end of the line before Linc said, "Is it really you? Not voice mail?"

"My mailbox is full thanks to you."

"So you got my messages."

"Yes. Did you get mine about terminating my contract with you?" Rose saw her lawyer nodding approval.

"Which one? The condo work or divorce papers?" Linc sounded ticked off. "I just got them from my lawyer with your signature."

"Good." Something inside her came apart and it was all she could do to get out a single word in a normal tone. She took a deep breath, then added, "So that's done. About the design contract—"

"That's not why I called."

"Oh? As far as I'm concerned there's nothing more to say."

"I couldn't disagree more."

Rose heard something in his voice that tugged at her heart, but giving in to the weakness was just asking for more trouble. That's the last thing she needed. "Linc, the only thing we could possibly have to discuss is why I'm unable to fulfill my legal obligation to decorate your condo—"

"Screw the contract. I don't give a damn about that."

"Glad to hear it. Thanks for calling and—" She was about to say "have a good life and don't ever darken my door again." Instead she added, "I'll watch for the final divorce papers with your signature."

"Everything is not even close to being settled."

She heard a deep, dark element in his voice and could picture intensity in his eyes. Her heart started to pound. "Linc, I can't—"

"I need to talk to you, Rose. Face-to-face. I'll come by and… There's a lot I have to tell you."

"No. I'll expect to receive a copy of the divorce papers. Goodbye, Linc." She tapped the end button and felt her anger go poof just before the pain rushed in.

"Way to keep it all about business," Vicki said.

"I tried. But it's always been personal with Linc."

The dam of feelings burst and Rose buried her face in her hands and started to cry. Damn him for doing this to her again.

Chapter Fifteen

After Rose hung up on him Linc stared at his cell phone and had the sinking feeling that he'd lost her forever. He was like his biological father, always losing at love. But unlike Robert Pierce, a lifetime of unhappiness would be his own fault. She could have been his but he blew it, as his sister said, by going all lone wolf.

Now what?

He left his Dallas condo and drove around for a while, somehow ending up in his parents' upscale suburban neighborhood. They probably didn't want to talk to him any more than his sister or Rose, but this was where he'd come all his life to get his head on straight. This time, them talking wasn't required when he apologized for being a jerk. All they had to do was listen.

Once he'd pulled his SUV into the semicircular driveway, he exited the vehicle and walked to the double-door entry of the impressive redbrick mansion. There was light coming through the glass panes so he rang the bell and waited long enough to wonder if he was deliberately being ignored. Not that they weren't justified, but he wasn't in the mood for this.

Then the outside porch light went on and his father opened the door. "Linc. Come in."

"Thanks."

The house hadn't changed since he'd last seen it. A crystal chandelier glittered from the ceiling of the two-story entryway and a circular table holding an impressive fresh bouquet of flowers sat on it.

"Your mother is in the family room." Hastings didn't hesitate and there was no surprise in his voice. No indication of resentment toward Linc for being a jackass.

When Hastings headed for the stairs and it looked as if he was going up, Linc said, "I'd like to talk to you and Mom both. If that's okay."

"All right." The older man led the way to the back of the house with its spacious, state-of-the-art kitchen and family-room combination. The ten-foot-high wall of windows looked out on the pool in the backyard and a golf course beyond. Nighttime lights illuminated the impressive view.

Katherine was sitting in a floral-patterned club chair reading a book. The Dallas newspapers were spread out on the leather corner group sitting in front of the formal fireplace and flat-screen TV above it. The scene brought an instant flash of familiarity and warmth. He'd missed it more than he would let himself acknowledge and regretted the time that could never be recovered. He also knew how the prodigal son must have felt.

"Lincoln." His mother stood and put down her book on the ottoman. She walked over to him and wrapped her arms around him tight. "It's good to see you."

"You, too." And it really was, even though it had only been a short time since that night in Ellie's kitchen. But he knew she meant it was good to see him *here*.

Katherine gave him one last firm squeeze before backing away. There was a puzzled expression on her face. "I don't mean to sound critical or ungrateful that you've come for a visit. But why are you here?"

"Several reasons. I need advice." He looked at his father specifically.

"Happy to help. And I'm touched. More than you'll ever know." He put his big hand on Linc's shoulder.

"I appreciate that, even though I don't deserve it. You have absolutely no reason to be gracious to me after the way I've behaved—"

"Let me stop you right there," Hastings said. "I love you. And I'm not going to qualify that statement by adding like my own son." The man's eyes were fierce with protective paternal pride and affection. "You *are* my son. And I have always tried to be the best father I knew how to be."

"You're the best dad in the world—" Linc's throat grew thick with emotion and he moved closer to embrace the good man who'd taught him to be a good man. "Thanks, Dad."

Hastings hugged him back, then cleared his throat as he stepped away. There was a suspicious moisture in his eyes. "Okay, then—"

"Mom, Dad—" Linc blew out a long breath as he looked at each of them. "I want to apologize to you both for turning my back on you and being a stubborn ass. It was not my finest hour and I deeply regret hurting you both. You didn't deserve that kind of treatment and I'm more sorry than you'll ever know."

"I wish I could tell you I wasn't hurt," his mother said,

"but that would be a lie. Still, I'm so very happy to see you and accept your apology."

"As easy as that? You're not going to make me grovel?"

Katherine shook her head. "It was very painful to see you confused, hurt, angry and blaming me. But the joy I have right this second at this reconciliation is in direct proportion to the love I have for you. It's never-ending and unconditional."

"I don't deserve it."

"Of course you do." She brushed off his denial.

"What made you come around?" Hastings asked.

"Yes," his mother chimed in. "How did this change of heart happen?"

Rose, he thought. When she said she loved him. At first he was frustrated and angry that he'd broken his vow and compromised her. Then some primal instinct took over and he was tired to the bone of not having the answers he needed to move forward with her. He knew he had to deal with the past first.

"I took your advice, Mom." He met his father's gaze. "Dad, I don't want to hurt you, but it's best to be up front. I went to see Robert Pierce."

"It's about damn time, son," Hastings said.

Linc couldn't help smiling. "Wow, okay then. You're not upset."

"How did it go?" His mother looked protective, wary.

"It sounds weird to say great, but it was. He's not the monster I'd made him out to be."

"And by hereditary extension that made you not a monster, too," Katherine said.

"Yeah. He just had the bad luck to fall in love with someone who wasn't free to love him back."

Hastings slipped his arm around his wife's waist. "He's

a fine man, Linc. Smart. Ethical. An excellent attorney and businessman. Pillar of the community."

"I should have gone to see him a long time ago." Before he'd left Rose the first time. His own stubbornness and stupidity made him want to put his fist through a wall. The colossal waste…

"You still haven't explained what made you go now."

Linc looked at his mother. "Something tells me you already have a pretty good idea."

"I have a theory," she confirmed.

"If it involves Rose, you'd be right. She said I was acting like a twelve-year-old. That there's room in my life for all family. She didn't know her father and I was lucky enough to have two."

"A very insightful young woman," Hastings said.

"One of many sterling qualities," Linc confirmed. His chest squeezed tight at the thought that he might never be able to make things right with her.

"So, you needed to see your biological father and make sure he isn't a despicable human being before setting your cap for her, as they say." His father nodded understanding.

"In my head it sounded much nobler than that," he admitted, "but essentially that is correct."

"So you've come to ask our advice about how to propose to Rose." Katherine's eyes sparkled with excitement at the scent of romance in the air.

"Technically I don't have to propose since we're not divorced."

His mother frowned. "Why do I get the feeling this visit is groveling practice? For seeing Rose?"

"Look, you guys, I've made mistakes in my life but this one is off the charts. And I don't know how to fix it." He explained to them about old habits kicking in, his leaving and her refusal to even talk to him now. "I have no idea what to do. How did you guys get past what happened when you were separated?"

Hastings smiled at his wife. "When you love someone, you forgive them. It's that simple."

"I'm not sure Rose can forgive me. The mistake I made is really big."

"Then the apology needs to be big, too," his father said thoughtfully. "This might be hard to understand, but you brought Katherine and I together."

He remembered his mother saying that and still couldn't wrap his mind around it. "But I was a mistake."

"I never want to hear you say that again," his mother said sternly. "You were then, and always will be, a blessing."

"Sorry, Mom. I really wasn't being that spoiled brat again. Just talking out loud." Linc looked at his father. "And I think I get where you're coming from, Dad. Use the personal flaw and turn it into a win."

Hastings beamed at him. "That's my boy."

"I'm glad you two are on the same testosterone wavelength," his mother said. "But can you translate that for little ol' me?"

"I'm still working on the plan," Linc said, "but I'll let you know how it all comes together."

He was going to do something big and bold to win Rose back. If it took the rest of his life he would show her that he'd never walk away from her again.

Rose closed up Tucker Designs for the night and walked up the stairs to her apartment on the building's second floor. She was a little more hopeful about her business after landing a wealthy client who wanted a recently purchased mansion in Highland Park decorated. It was a Dallas suburb where tech and oil millionaires lived and that made her a little suspicious that Linc might have sent her the client. Because he'd been sending other stuff, too.

She unlocked her door, then opened it and walked inside, taking a deep breath to smell the sweet floral fragrance that filled the apartment. There were rose-filled vases everywhere. Beautiful lavender roses. White ones blushing pink. Yellow and coral. Just gorgeous. But looking at them made her heart hurt because of how much she missed Linc.

She missed talking, teasing and laughing with him. She loved him and this apology with flowers was so tempting. How was she supposed to resist that? But how could she let herself trust him? It would destroy her to let her guard down and be abandoned again. There wouldn't just be heart damage; she would need to have her head examined.

Her cell phone rang and she pulled it from the pocket of her slacks and checked caller ID. It was Linc again. Her rational self warned her not to answer but the emotional part of her ignored it. Time to make that shrink appointment, she thought, after hitting the talk button.

"Linc, please, I'm begging you to leave me alone."

"Do you like the flowers?"

His voice, the deep smoothness of it, slid inside and squeezed her heart. This was absolute torture. Like having red velvet cupcakes in the house while struggling to lose that last five stubborn pounds.

And who didn't like flowers, for Pete's sake? Unless you were allergic to them. She was allergic to Linc; he was bad for her and made her eyes water.

"Rose?"

"The flowers are beautiful," she finally said.

"Which color is your favorite?"

It was on the tip of her tongue to say lavender, then she realized he was effortlessly sucking her into his web. "My favorite is of no concern to you. I'm not speaking to you anymore. We have nothing more to talk about."

She ended the call and realized her cheeks were wet from tears. See? Allergic to Linc. The best way to live with it was *not* to live with it. No matter how much she wanted to.

The doorbell rang, startling her out of the "allergy" attack, and she brushed the moisture from her cheeks. If this was another florist delivering flowers from Linc...

She opened the door. It wasn't a delivery person, but the sender himself with a cell phone in one hand and the handle of a wheeled suitcase in the other. *Speechless* didn't even begin to describe how she felt.

"Hi." Without waiting for an invitation he walked inside, as brazen as could be, and shut the door behind him. As if he was staying.

That loosened her tongue. "What are you doing?"

"I'm moving in. Where should I put my stuff?"

"You can't be serious."

"And yet, I am," he said cheerfully.

"This is my place and I most definitely did not invite you into it."

He looked around and nodded with satisfaction at the vases covering every flat surface in the room. "The flowers look great. Not that this place needs them. It's perfect because of your special touch."

Her heart began a steady pounding against the inside of her chest. "I want you to leave, Linc. Now."

"No, you don't."

"You have no right to tell me what I want. No right to come into my home and demand a drawer. You walked away from me. Twice. And we're divorced. I signed the papers."

"That reminds me." He snapped his fingers and pulled

a familiar-looking manila envelope from an outside pocket of his suitcase. He held it out. "Here are the papers you signed."

She lifted the flap and reached inside, expecting a packet of papers but instead pulling out confetti. Her gaze shot to his. "This is shredded."

"I know."

"How could you do that?"

"There's this handy machine and you just feed the paper in and it comes out like that." He shrugged. "Easy."

"You know that's not what I meant." Rose stared at him. "I don't understand."

"Short version? I instructed my attorney not to file the papers with the court. We're still a little bit married."

"That's not the part I don't get," she said through gritted teeth. The urge to brain him with a vase of flowers was strong in her. "Why didn't you sign them? I thought you wanted to divorce me."

"Not you." His expression turned serious for the first time. "I wanted to divorce my past. My biological father and the reality of not actually being born a Hart. I wanted to be the man you thought you married."

"You are," she protested.

"I get that now and I've come to terms with the person I am. Thanks to you and my parents."

"What happened?" She set the envelope containing shredded legal documents on her coffee table.

"I took your suggestion and saw my father." He slid his fingertips into the pockets of his jeans. "He's a decent man who is a victim of tragic love. It's a 'good news, bad news' thing. The bad is he's been married and divorced a few times but it's because he's trying to find a woman like my mother."

"So he's a one-woman man," Rose ventured.

"Exactly."

"You were afraid you'd inherited the player gene from him," she said.

"Yes." He smiled a little uncertainly. "I didn't want to put you through being married to a womanizing jerk."

"You never were that guy," she said again.

"But I didn't know that I wouldn't turn into him. And I couldn't take the chance. Not with you. I'd rather live with the pain of not having you than risk hurting you."

Her heart was melting as surely as ice cream in the sun. "And now?"

"It seems I do take after him, at least in one way."

"Oh?"

"Yeah." He took a step closer, his gaze never leaving hers. "I fell in love with you. You're the only woman for me and there will never be anyone else."

"I can't, Linc—" Emotion choked off her words and she looked away.

"I know I've hurt you and you'll never know how sorry I am for that. But you and I are meant to be together. The universe is telling us so. Look at all the signs. There was no divorce. You never found anyone else and neither did I."

"Linc…" She met his gaze and recognized the intensity of desperation in his eyes.

"Do you know why neither of us connected with someone else? I can only speak for myself, but I'd wager my last dollar that the same is true for you. In fact you told me that you'd never stopped loving me. And I didn't know what to do."

"Talk to me maybe?"

"I get that now and I'm working on my communication skills. Starting with this—I love you, Rose. I always have. There will never be anyone else for me. Unlike my father, I met the woman of my dreams and was lucky enough to marry her. It was the smartest thing I ever did. After that I—" He shrugged. "Stupid mistake after stupid mistake. The best I can say is that my motives were pure. I was simply trying to protect you from the mess of my life. I just hope you can forgive me. Be my wife. Don't condemn me to a life without you in it."

"Oh, Linc—" She caught the corner of her bottom lip between her teeth.

"Before you give me your final answer, you should know that I won't give up. If you won't let me move in here, I'll pitch a tent outside. I'll send flowers, rent advertising space on I-35 proclaiming my love. Along with a plug for your decorating business."

"What about your business in Blackwater Lake?"

"I'll commute. The condo will stay a shell unless you work your magic. No one but you will ever decorate it." He looked down for a moment, then stared into her eyes. "If you can find it in your heart to give me another chance, I swear that I will never give you a reason to regret it."

Rose had never seen him so vulnerable, so not in control of his feelings. That was new and filled her heart with hope. And most importantly, trust.

She took a step closer and could feel the heat of his body even though they weren't touching. "Can I have my job back?"

"Being my wife?" He frowned.

"No." She glanced down at the envelope on the table, then toyed with the button on his crisp, white shirt. "I never quit being married to you. I was talking about decorating your condo. And living there together."

He closed his eyes for a moment and let out a long breath before looking at her again. A small smile turned up the corners of his mouth as he nodded. "With your special touch, it will be like having the essence of you wrapped around me. To my way of thinking that's about as close to heaven on earth as a man can get."

"I love you, Lincoln Hart."

"Words with wow factor." He grinned, then pulled her into his arms and kissed her into more than being just a little bit married.

* * * * *

Return to Blackwater Lake in August 2017,
when Faith Connelly and Sam Hart are forced
together by raging wild fires in the next book in
THE BACHELORS OF BLACKWATER LAKE
miniseries!

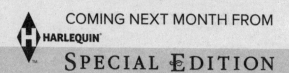
#2539 FINDING OUR FOREVER
Silver Springs • by Brenda Novak
When Cora Kelly gets a job at the boys' ranch run by her birth mother, Aiyana Turner, she thinks she has a year to get to know her mother without revealing her identity. But she never thought she'd fall in love with Aiyana's adopted son, Eli. Once that happens, she's forced to broaden the lie—or risk telling a very unwelcome truth.

#2540 FROM FORTUNE TO FAMILY MAN
The Fortunes of Texas: The Secret Fortunes • by Judy Duarte
Kieran Fortune becomes an instant father to a three-year-old when his best friend dies in a ranch accident. Dana Trevino, his friend's ex-girlfriend, steps in to help the floundering single dad, only to find herself falling for a man she considers way out of her league!

#2541 MEANT TO BE MINE
Matchmaking Mamas • by Marie Ferrarella
First they were playground pals and then college rivals. Now Tiffany Lee and Eddie Montoya are both teachers at Los Naranjos Elementary School, and it looks like the old rivalry may be heating up to be something more when their classrooms go head-to-head in the annual school charity run.

#2542 MARRIED TO THE MOM-TO-BE
The Cedar River Cowboys • by Helen Lacey
Kayla Rickard knew falling in love with Liam O'Sullivan broke the rules of the bitter feud between their families, and she thought she could keep their impromptu marriage a secret. That was, until her pregnancy changed everything!

#2543 THE GROOM'S LITTLE GIRLS
Proposals in Paradise • by Katie Meyer
Dani Post was on the fast track to success before tragedy left her craving the security and routine of home. But when she falls for a handsome widower and his twin girls, she realizes she must face her past if she's going to have any chance of making them her future.

#2544 THE PRINCESS PROBLEM
Drake Diamonds • by Teri Wilson
Handsome diamond heir Dalton Drake struck a royal bargain to give shelter to Aurélie Marchand, a runaway princess in New York City, but falling in love was never part of the deal!

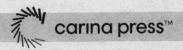
Ben handed Laney a sealed envelope, then walked around the back of the partial chair. "Quite a project you've got here."

"I probably should have taken a nap after the first one." She peeled the flap off the envelope and pulled out a folded paper.

Inside was a short, handwritten note. *I think you should go for it.*

All of a sudden, her cheeks felt warm and she wanted to hide the words against her chest or crumple the paper so there was no chance Ben could read it, even though he'd probably have no idea what her cousin meant by it. Instead she refolded the paper and slid it back into the envelope. Then she pressed the flap down the best she could before lifting the toolbox and sliding it underneath.

"Everything okay?" he asked.

"Yeah." She looked up at him, her mind flailing for some reasonable explanation why Nola would ask Ben to deliver something to her. "Just some information I needed about getting a Maine driver's license and plates for my car and... stuff."

Please don't ask me why she didn't just call or text the information, she thought as soon as the words left her mouth.

"Cool. Do you need some help with this chair?"

"No, thank you. I've got it."

"Want some company?"

"Sure." She wondered if he'd make it five minutes before he leaned in and tried to tighten a bolt for her before just building the rest of it himself. "Want a drink?"

He held up an insulated tumbler as he sat in her folding camp chair, shaking it so the ice rattled. "I have one, thanks. Do you need a fresh one?"

Laney kept her face down, looking at the instruction sheet, so he wouldn't see her smile. He was so polite, but she didn't want to imagine him in her camper. He wasn't as tall as Josh, but he had broad shoulders and she could picture him filling the space. If they were both in there, they'd brush against each other trying to get by…and her imagination needed to change the subject before she started blushing again.

"No, thanks," she said. "I'm good."

"Okay. Yesterday's accident aside, how are you liking the Northern Star? And Whitford in general, I guess."

"I haven't seen too much of Whitford yet. The market and gas station, and the hardware store. And obviously I'll be going to the town hall soon."

"You haven't eaten at the Trailside Diner yet?"

"No, but Nola brought me a sandwich from there yesterday. Right before the accident. It was really good."

"Their dinner menu is even better."

Was he working his way around to asking her out to dinner? It had been so long since she'd dated, she wasn't sure if she was reading too much into a friendly conversation. But it seemed her next line would naturally be *I'll have to try it sometime* and then he'd say *How about tomorrow night?* or something like that.

And she had no idea how she felt about that.

Don't miss
WHAT IT TAKES:
A KOWALSKI REUNION NOVEL
by Shannon Stacey, available wherever books are sold.

www.CarinaPress.com

JUST CAN'T GET ENOUGH?

Join our social communities
and talk to us online.

You will have access to the latest
news on upcoming titles and special
promotions, but most importantly,
you can talk to other fans about your
favorite Harlequin reads.

Harlequin.com/Community

Facebook.com/HarlequinBooks

Twitter.com/HarlequinBooks

Pinterest.com/HarlequinBooks